THE PELICAN SHAKESPEARE

GENERAL EDITOR ALFRED HARBAGE

THE TEMPEST

WILLIAM SHAKESPEARE

THE TEMPEST

EDITED BY NORTHROP FRYE

PENGUIN BOOKS

PENGUIN BOOKS
Published by the Penguin Group
Penguin Books USA Inc.,
375 Hudson Street, New York, New York 10014, U.S.A.
Penguin Books Ltd, 27 Wrights Lane, London W8 5TZ, England
Penguin Books Australia Ltd, Ringwood, Victoria, Australia
Penguin Books Canada Ltd, 10 Alcorn Avenue,
Toronto, Ontario, Canada M4V 3B2
Penguin Books (N.Z.) Ltd, 182–190 Wairau Road,
Auckland 10, New Zealand

Penguin Books Ltd, Registered Offices:
Harmondsworth, Middlesex, England

First published in *The Pelican Shakespeare* 1959
This revised edition first published 1970

31 33 35 37 39 40 38 36 34 32

Library of Congress catalog card number: 76-95582
ISBN 0 14 0714.15 4

Printed in the United States of America by
Set in Monotype Ehrhardt

CONTENTS

PUBLISHER'S NOTE

Soon after the thirty-eight volumes forming *The Pelican Shake-speare* had been published, they were brought together in *The Complete Pelican Shakespeare*. The editorial revisions and new textual features are explained in detail in the General Editor's Preface to the one-volume edition. They have all been incorporated in the present volume. The following should be mentioned in particular:

The lines are not numbered in arbitrary units. Instead all lines are numbered which contain a word, phrase, or allusion explained in the glossarial notes. In the occasional instances where there is a long stretch of unannotated text, certain lines are numbered in italics to serve the conventional reference purpose.

The intrusive and often inaccurate place-headings inserted by early editors are omitted (as is becoming standard practise), but for the convenience of those who miss them, an indication of locale now appears as first item in the annotation of each scene.

In the interest of both elegance and utility, each speech-prefix is set in a separate line when the speaker's lines are in verse, except when these words form the second half of a pentameter line. Thus the verse form of the speech is kept visually intact, and turned-over lines are avoided. What is printed as verse and what is printed as prose has, in general, the authority of the original texts. Departures from the original texts in this regard have only the authority of editorial tradition and the judgment of the Pelican editors; and, in a few instances, are admittedly arbitrary.

SHAKESPEARE AND
HIS STAGE

William Shakespeare was christened in Holy Trinity Church, Stratford-upon-Avon, April 26, 1564. His birth is traditionally assigned to April 23. He was the eldest of four boys and two girls who survived infancy in the family of John Shakespeare, glover and trader of Henley Street, and his wife Mary Arden, daughter of a small landowner of Wilmcote. In 1568 John was elected Bailiff (equivalent to Mayor) of Stratford, having already filled the minor municipal offices. The town maintained for the sons of the burgesses a free school, taught by a university graduate and offering preparation in Latin sufficient for university entrance; its early registers are lost, but there can be little doubt that Shakespeare received the formal part of his education in this school.

On November 27, 1582, a license was issued for the marriage of William Shakespeare (aged eighteen) and Ann Hathaway (aged twenty-six), and on May 26, 1583, their child Susanna was christened in Holy Trinity Church. The inference that the marriage was forced upon the youth is natural but not inevitable; betrothal was legally binding at the time, and was sometimes regarded as conferring conjugal rights. Two additional children of the marriage, the twins Hamnet and Judith, were christened on February 2, 1585. Meanwhile the prosperity of the elder Shakespeares had declined, and William was impelled to seek a career outside Stratford.

The tradition that he spent some time as a country

teacher is old but unverifiable. Because of the absence of records his early twenties are called the "lost years," and only one thing about them is certain – that at least some of these years were spent in winning a place in the acting profession. He may have begun as a provincial trouper, but by 1592 he was established in London and prominent enough to be attacked. In a pamphlet of that year, *Groats-worth of Wit*, the ailing Robert Greene complained of the neglect which university writers like himself had suffered from actors, one of whom was daring to set up as a playwright:

. . . an vpstart Crow, beautified with our feathers, that with his *Tygers hart wrapt in a Players hyde*, supposes he is as well able to bombast out a blanke verse as the best of you: and beeing an absolute *Iohannes fac totum*, is in his owne conceit the onely Shake-scene in a countrey.

The pun on his name, and the parody of his line "O tiger's heart wrapped in a woman's hide" (*3 Henry VI*), pointed clearly to Shakespeare. Some of his admirers protested, and Henry Chettle, the editor of Greene's pamphlet, saw fit to apologize:

. . . I am as sory as if the originall fault had beene my fault, because my selfe haue seene his demeanor no lesse ciuill than he excelent in the qualitie he professes: Besides, diuers of worship haue reported his vprightnes of dealing, which argues his honesty, and his facetious grace in writting, that approoues his Art. (Prefatory epistle, *Kind-Harts Dreame*)

The plague closed the London theatres for many months in 1592–94, denying the actors their livelihood. To this period belong Shakespeare's two narrative poems, *Venus and Adonis* and *The Rape of Lucrece*, both dedicated to the Earl of Southampton. No doubt the poet was rewarded with a gift of money as usual in such cases, but he did no further dedicating and we have no reliable information on whether Southampton, or anyone else, became his regular patron. His sonnets, first mentioned in 1598 and published without his consent in 1609, are intimate without being explicitly autobiographical. They seem to commemorate the poet's friendship with an idealized youth, rivalry with a more favored poet, and love affair with a dark mistress; and his bitterness when the mistress betrays him in conjunction with the friend; but it is difficult to decide precisely what the "story" is, impossible to decide whether it is fictional or true. The true distinction of the sonnets, at least of those not purely conventional, rests in the universality of the thoughts and moods they express, and in their poignancy and beauty.

In 1594 was formed the theatrical company known until 1603 as the Lord Chamberlain's men, thereafter as the King's men. Its original membership included, besides Shakespeare, the beloved clown Will Kempe and the famous actor Richard Burbage. The company acted in various London theatres and even toured the provinces, but it is chiefly associated in our minds with the Globe Theatre built on the south bank of the Thames in 1599. Shakespeare was an actor and joint owner of this company (and its Globe) through the remainder of his creative years. His plays, written at the average rate of two a year, together with Burbage's acting won it its place of leadership among the London companies.

Individual plays began to appear in print, in editions both honest and piratical, and the publishers became increasingly aware of the value of Shakespeare's name on the title pages. As early as 1598 he was hailed as the leading English dramatist in the *Palladis Tamia* of Francis Meres:

As *Plautus* and *Seneca* are accounted the best for Comedy and Tragedy among the Latines, so *Shakespeare* among the English is the most excellent in both kinds for the stage: for Comedy, witnes his *Gentlemen of Verona*, his *Errors*, his *Loue labors lost*, his *Loue labours wonne* [at one time in print but no longer extant, at least under this title], his *Midsummers night dream*, & his *Merchant of Venice*; for Tragedy, his *Richard the 2*, *Richard the 3*, *Henry the 4*, *King Iohn*, *Titus Andronicus*, and his *Romeo and Iuliet*.

The note is valuable both in indicating Shakespeare's prestige and in helping us to establish a chronology. In the second half of his writing career, history plays gave place to the great tragedies; and farces and light comedies gave place to the problem plays and symbolic romances. In 1623, seven years after his death, his former fellow-actors, John Heminge and Henry Condell, cooperated with a group of London printers in bringing out his plays in collected form. The volume is generally known as the First Folio.

Shakespeare had never severed his relations with Stratford. His wife and children may sometimes have shared his London lodgings, but their home was Stratford. His son Hamnet was buried there in 1596, and his daughters Susanna and Judith were married there in 1607 and 1616 respectively. (His father, for whom he had secured a coat of arms and thus the privilege of writing himself gentleman, died in 1601, his mother in 1608.) His considerable earnings in London, as actor-sharer, part owner of the Globe, and playwright, were invested chiefly in Stratford property. In 1597 he purchased for £60 New Place, one of the two most imposing residences in the town. A number of other business transactions, as well as minor episodes in his career, have left documentary records. By 1611 he was in a position to retire, and he seems gradually to have withdrawn from theatrical activity in order to live in Stratford. In March, 1616, he made a will, leaving token bequests to Burbage, Heminge, and Condell, but the bulk of his estate to his family. The most famous feature of the will, the bequest of the second-best bed to his wife, reveals nothing about Shakespeare's marriage; the quaintness of the provision seems commonplace to those familiar with ancient testaments. Shakespeare died April 23, 1616, and was buried in the Stratford church where he had been christened. Within seven years a monument was erected to his memory on the north wall of the chancel. Its portrait bust and the Droeshout engraving on the title page of the First Folio provide the only likenesses with an established claim to authenticity. The best verbal vignette was written by his rival Ben Jonson, the more impressive for being imbedded in a context mainly critical :

... I loved the man, and doe honour his memory (on this side idolatry) as much as any. Hee was indeed honest, and of an open and free nature: had an excellent Phantsie, brave notions, and gentle expressions.... (*Timber or Discoveries*, ca. 1623–30)

*

The reader of Shakespeare's plays is aided by a general knowledge of the way in which they were staged. The King's men acquired a roofed and artificially lighted theatre only toward the close of Shakespeare's career, and then only for winter use. Nearly all his plays were designed for performance in such structures as the Globe – a three-tiered amphitheatre with a large rectangular platform extending to the center of its yard. The plays were staged by daylight, by large casts brilliantly costumed, but with only a minimum of properties, without scenery, and quite possibly without intermissions. There was a rear stage gallery for action "above," and a curtained rear recess for "discoveries" and other special effects, but by far the major portion of any play was enacted upon the projecting platform, with episode following episode in swift succession, and with shifts of time and place signaled the audience only by the momentary clearing of the stage between the episodes. Information about the identity of the characters and, when necessary, about the time and place of the action was incorporated in the dialogue. No place-headings have been inserted in the present editions; these are apt to obscure the original fluidity of structure, with the emphasis upon action and speech rather than scenic background. (Indications of place are supplied in the footnotes.) The acting, including that of the youthful apprentices to the profession who performed the parts of women, was highly skillful, with a premium placed upon grace of gesture and beauty of diction. The audiences, a cross section of the general public, commonly numbered a thousand, sometimes more than two thousand. Judged by the type of plays they applauded, these audiences were not only large but also perceptive.

THE TEXTS OF THE PLAYS

About half of Shakespeare's plays appeared in print for the first time in the folio volume of 1623. The others had been published individually, usually in quarto volumes, during his lifetime or in the six years following his death. The copy used by the printers of the quartos varied greatly in merit, sometimes representing Shakespeare's true text, sometimes only a debased version of that text. The copy used by the printers of the folio also varied in merit, but was chosen with care. Since it consisted of the best available manuscripts, or the more acceptable quartos (although frequently in editions other than the first), or of quartos corrected by reference to manuscripts, we have good or reasonably good texts of most of the thirty-seven plays.

In the present series, the plays have been newly edited from quarto or folio texts, depending, when a choice offered, upon which is now regarded by bibliographical specialists as the more authoritative. The ideal has been to reproduce the chosen texts with as few alterations as possible, beyond occasional relineation, expansion of abbreviations, and modernization of punctuation and spelling. Emendation is held to a minimum, and such material as has been added, in the way of stage directions and lines supplied by an alternative text, has been enclosed in square brackets.

None of the plays printed in Shakespeare's lifetime were divided into acts and scenes, and the inference is that the author's own manuscripts were not so divided. In the folio collection, some of the plays remained undivided, some were divided into acts, and some were divided into acts and scenes. During the eighteenth century all of the plays were divided into acts and scenes, and in the Cambridge edition of the mid-nineteenth century, from which the influential Globe text derived, this division was more or less regularized and the lines were numbered. Many useful works of reference employ the act–scene–line apparatus thus established.

Since this act–scene division is obviously convenient, but is of very dubious authority so far as Shakespeare's own structural principles are concerned, or the original manner of staging his plays, a problem is presented to modern editors. In the present series the act–scene division is retained marginally, and may be viewed as a reference aid like the line numbering. A star marks the points of division when these points have been determined by a cleared stage indicating a shift of time and place in the action of the play, or when no harm results from the editorial assumption that there is such a shift. However, at those points where the established division is clearly misleading – that is, where continuous action has been split up into separate "scenes" – the star is omitted and the distortion corrected. This mechanical expedient seemed the best means of combining utility and accuracy.

THE GENERAL EDITOR

INTRODUCTION

In the opening scene of *The Tempest* there is not only a
sinking ship but a dissolving society. The storm, like the
storm in *King Lear*, does not care that it is afflicting a king,
and Gonzalo's protests about the deference due to royalty
seem futile enough. But while everyone is unreasonable,
we can distinguish Gonzalo, who is ready to meet his fate
with some detachment and humor, from Antonio and
Sebastian, who are merely screaming abuse at the sailors
trying to save their lives. The boatswain, who comes so
vividly to life in a few crisp lines, dominates this scene and
leaves us with a strong sense of the superiority of personal
character to social rank.

The shipwrecked characters are then divided by Ariel
into three main groups: Ferdinand; the Court Party proper; Stephano and Trinculo. Each goes through a pursuit
of illusions, an ordeal, and a symbolic vision. The Court
Party hunts for Ferdinand with strange shapes appearing
and vanishing around them; their ordeal is a labyrinth of
"forthrights and meanders" in which they founder with
exhaustion, and to them is presented the vision of the dis-
appearing banquet, symbolic of deceitful desires. There
follows confinement and a madness which brings them to
conviction of sin, self-knowledge, and repentance. Like
Hamlet, Prospero delays revenge and sets up a dramatic
action to catch the conscience of a king; like Lear on a
small scale, Alonso is a king who gains in dignity by suf-
fering. The search of Stephano and Trinculo for Prospero

is also misled by illusions; their ordeal is a horse-pond and their symbolic vision the "trumpery" dangled in front of them. What happens to them is external and physical rather than internal and mental: they are hunted by hounds, filled with cramps, and finally reach what might be called a conviction of inadequacy. Probably they then settle into their old roles again: if a cold-blooded sneering assassin like Antonio can be forgiven, these amusing and fundamentally likeable rascals can be too. Ferdinand, being the hero, has a better time: he is led by Ariel's music to Miranda, undergoes the ordeal of the log pile, where he takes over Caliban's role as a bearer of wood, and his symbolic vision is that of the wedding masque.

The characters thus appear to be taking their appropriate places in a new kind of social order. We soon realize that the island looks different to different people – it is a pleasanter place to Gonzalo than to Antonio or Sebastian – and that each one is stimulated to exhibit his own ideal of society. At one end, Ferdinand unwillingly resigns himself to becoming King of Naples by the death of Alonso; at the other, Sebastian plots to become King of Naples by murdering Alonso. In between come Stephano, whose ambition to be king of the island is more ridiculous but somehow less despicable than Sebastian's, and Gonzalo, who dreams of a primitive golden age of equality and leisure, not very adequate as a social theory, but simple and honest, full of good nature and good will, like Gonzalo himself.

Into the midst of this society comes the islander Caliban, who is, on one level of nature, a natural man, a primitive whose name seems to echo the "cannibals" of Montaigne's famous essay. He is not a cannibal, but his existence in the play forms an ironic comment on Gonzalo's reverie, which has been taken from a passage in the same essay. Caliban is a human being, as Ariel is not; and whatever he does, Prospero feels responsible for him: "this thing of darkness I / Acknowledge mine," Prospero says. Whether or not he is, as one hopeful critic suggested, an anticipation of Darwin's "missing link," he knows he is not like the apes "With foreheads villainous low"; his sensuality is haunted by troubled dreams of beauty; he is not taken in by the "trumpery," and we leave him with his mind on higher things. His ambitions are to kill Prospero and rape Miranda, both, considering his situation, eminently natural desires; and even these he resigns to Stephano, to whom he tries to be genuinely loyal. Nobody has a good word for Caliban: he is a born devil to Prospero, an abhorred slave to Miranda, and to others not obviously his superiors either in intelligence or virtue he is a puppy-headed monster, a mooncalf, and a plain fish. Yet he has his own dignity, and he is certainly no Yahoo, for all his ancient and fishlike smell. True, Shakespeare, like Swift, clearly does not assume that the natural man on Caliban's level is capable also of a reasonable life. But he has taken pains to make Caliban as memorable and vivid as any character in the play.

As a natural man, Caliban is *mere* nature, nature without nurture, as Prospero would say: the nature that manifests itself more as an instinctive propensity to evil than as the calculated criminality of Antonio and Sebastian, which is rationally corrupted nature. But to an Elizabethan poet "nature" had an upper level, a cosmic and moral order that may be entered through education, obedience to law, and the habit of virtue. In this expanded sense we may say that the whole society being formed on the island under Prospero's guidance is a natural society. Its top level is represented by Miranda, whose chastity and innocence put her, like her poetic descendant the Lady in *Comus*, in tune with the harmony of a higher nature. The discipline necessary to live in this higher nature is imposed on the other characters by Prospero's magic. In Shakespeare's day the occult arts, especially alchemy, whose language Prospero is using at the beginning of the fifth act, were often employed as symbols of such discipline.

Shakespeare did not select Montaigne's essay on the cannibals as the basis for Gonzalo's "commonwealth" speech merely at random. Montaigne is no Rousseau: he is not talking about imaginary noble savages. He is saying that, despite their unconventional way of getting their proteins, cannibals have many virtues we have not, and if we pretend to greater virtues we ought to have at least theirs. They are not models for imitation; they are children of nature who can show us what is unnatural in our own lives. If we can understand that, we shall be wiser than the cannibals as well as wiser than our present selves. Prospero takes the society of Alonso's ship, immerses it in magic, and then sends it back to the world, its original ranks restored, but given a new wisdom in the light of which Antonio's previous behavior can be seen to be "unnatural." In the Epilogue Prospero hands over to the audience what his art has created, a vision of a society permeated by the virtues of tolerance and forgiveness, in the form of one of the most beautiful plays in the world. And, adds Prospero, you might start practising those virtues by applauding the play.

The Tempest is not an allegory, or a religious drama: if it were, Prospero's great "revels" speech would say, not merely that all earthly things will vanish, but that an eternal world will take their place. In a religious context, Prospero's renunciation of magic would represent the resigning of his will to a divine will, one that can do what the boatswain says Gonzalo cannot do, command the elements to silence and work the peace of the present. In Christianity the higher level of nature is God's original creation, from which man broke away with Adam's fall. It is usually symbolized by the music of the heavenly spheres, of which the one nearest us is the moon. The traditional conception of the magician was of one who could control the moon: this power is attributed to Sycorax, but it is a sinister power not associated with Prospero, whose magic and music belong to the sublunary world.

In the wedding masque of the fourth act and the recognition scene of the fifth, therefore, we find ourselves moving, not out of the world, but from an ordinary to a renewed and ennobled vision of nature. The masque shows the meeting of a fertile earth and a gracious sky introduced by the goddess of the rainbow, and leads up to a dance of nymphs representing the spring rains with reapers representing the autumnal harvest. The masque has about it the freshness of Noah's new world, after the tempest had receded and the rainbow promised that seedtime and harvest should not cease. There is thus a glimpse, as Ferdinand recognizes, of an Earthly Paradise, where, as in Milton's Eden, there is no winter but spring and autumn "Danced hand in hand." In the last act, as in *The Winter's Tale*, there is a curious pretense that some of the characters have died and are brought back to life. The discovery of Ferdinand is greeted by Sebastian, of all people, as "A most high miracle." But the miracles are those of a natural, and therefore also a moral and intellectual, renewal of life. Some of Shakespeare's romances feature a final revelation through a goddess or oracle, both of which Alonso expects, but in *The Tempest* goddess and oracle are represented by Miranda and Ariel (in his speech at the banquet) respectively. Ariel is a spirit of nature, and Miranda is a natural spirit, in other words a human being, greeting the "brave new world" in all the good faith of innocence.

Hence we distort the play if we think of Prospero as supernatural, just as we do if we think of Caliban as a devil. Prospero is a tempest-raiser like the witches in *Macbeth*, though morally at the opposite pole; he is a "white" magician. Anyone with Prospero's powers is an agent of fate, a cheating fate if evil, a benevolent fate or providence if motivated as he is. Great courage was required of all magicians, white or black, for the elemental spirits they controlled were both unwilling and malignant, and any sign of faltering meant terrible disaster. Ariel is loyal because of his debt of gratitude to Prospero, and because he is a very high-class spirit, too delicate to work for a black witch like Sycorax. But even he has a short memory, and has to be periodically reminded what his debt of gratitude is. Of the others Caliban says, probably with some truth, "They all do hate him / As rootedly as I." The nervous strain of dealing with such creatures shows up in Prospero's relations with human beings too; and in his tormenting of Caliban, in his lame excuse for making Ferdinand's wooing "uneasy," in his fussing over protecting Miranda from her obviously honorable lover, there is a touch of the busybody.

Still, his benevolence is genuine, and as far as the action of the play goes he seems an admirable ruler. Yet he appears to have been a remarkably incompetent Duke of Milan, and not to be promising much improvement after he returns. His talents are evidently dramatic rather than political, and he seems less of a practical magician plotting the discomfiture of his enemies than a creative artist calling spirits from their confines to enact his present fancies. It has often been thought that Prospero is a self-portrait of Shakespeare, and there may well be something in him of a harassed overworked actor-manager, scolding the lazy actors, praising the good ones in connoisseur's language, thinking up jobs for the idle, constantly aware of his limited time before his show goes on, his nerves tense and alert for breakdowns while it is going on, looking forward longingly to peaceful retirement, yet in the meantime having to go out and beg the audience for applause.

Prospero's magic, in any case, is an "art" which includes, in fact largely consists of, music and drama. Dramatists from Euripides to Pirandello have been fascinated by the paradox of reality and illusion in drama: the play is an illusion like the dream, and yet a focus of reality more intense than life affords. The action of *The Tempest* moves from sea to land, from chaos to new creation, from reality to realization. What seems at first illusory, the magic and music, becomes real, and the *Realpolitik* of Antonio and Sebastian becomes illusion. In this island the quality of one's dreaming is an index of character. When Antonio and Sebastian remain awake plotting murder, they show that they are the real dreamers, sunk in the hallucinations of greed. We find Stephano better company because his are the exuberant dreams of the stage boaster, as when he claims to have swum thirty-five leagues "off and on," when we know that he has floated to shore on a wine cask. Caliban's life is full of nightmare interspersed by strange gleams of ecstasy. When the Court Party first came to the island "no man was his own"; they had not found their "proper selves." Through the mirages of Ariel, the mops and mows of the other spirits, the vanities of Prospero's art, and the fevers of madness, reality grows up in them from inside, in response to the fertilizing influence of illusion.

Few plays are so haunted by the passing of time as *The Tempest*: it has derived even its name from a word (*tempestas*) which means time as well as tempest. Timing was important to a magician: everything depended on it when the alchemist's project gathered to a head; astrologers were exact observers of time ("The very minute bids thee ope thine ear," Prospero says to Miranda), and the most famous of all stories about magicians, the story told in Greene's play *Friar Bacon and Friar Bungay*, had the warning of "time is past" for its moral. The same preoccupation affects the other characters too, from the sailors in the storm to Ariel watching the clock for his freedom. The tide, which also waits for no man, ebbs and flows around this Mediterranean island in defiance of geography, and its imagery enters the plotting of Antonio and Sebastian and the grief of Ferdinand. When everyone is trying to make the most of his time, it seems strange that a melancholy elegy over the dissolving of all things in time should be the emotional crux of the play.

A very deliberate echo in the dialogue gives us the clue

to this. Morally, *The Tempest* shows a range of will extending from Prospero's self-control, which includes his control of all the other characters, to the self-abandonment of Alonso's despair, when, crazed with guilt and grief, he resolves to drown himself "deeper than e'er plummet sounded." Intellectually, it shows a range of vision extending from the realizing of a moment in time, the zenith of Prospero's fortune, which becomes everyone else's zenith too, to the sense of the nothingness of all temporal things. When Prospero renounces his magic, his "book" falls into the vanishing world, "deeper than did ever plummet sound." He has done what his art can do; he has held the mirror up to nature. Alonso and the rest are promised many explanations after the play is over, but we are left only with the darkening mirror, the visions fading and leaving not a rack behind. Once again the Epilogue reminds us that Prospero has used up all his magic in the play, and what more he can do depends on us.

It is not difficult to see, then, why so many students of Shakespeare, rightly or wrongly, have felt that *The Tempest* is in a peculiar sense Shakespeare's play, and that there is something in it of Shakespeare's farewell to his art. Two other features of it reinforce this feeling: the fact that no really convincing general source for the play has yet been discovered, and the fact that it is probably the last play wholly written by Shakespeare.

Whether a general source turns up or not, *The Tempest* is still erudite and allusive enough, full of echoes of literature, from the classics to the pamphlets of Shakespeare's own time. The scene of the play, an island somewhere between Tunis and Naples, suggests the journey of Aeneas from Carthage to Rome. Gonzalo's identification of Tunis and Carthage, and the otherwise tedious business about "Widow Dido" in the second act, seems almost to be emphasizing the parallel. Like *The Tempest*, the *Aeneid* begins with a terrible storm and goes on to tell a story of wanderings in which a banquet with harpies figures prominently. Near the route of Aeneas' journey, according to Virgil, was the abode of Circe, of whom (at least in her Renaissance form) Sycorax is a close relative. Circe suggests Medea, whose speech in Ovid's *Metamorphoses* is the model for Prospero's renunciation speech. Echoes from the shipwreck of St Paul (Ariel's phrase "Not a hair perished" recalls Acts xxvii, 34), from St Augustine, who also had associations with Carthage, and from Apuleius, with his interest in magic and initiation, are appropriate enough in such a play. Most of the traditional magical names of elemental spirits were of Hebrew origin, and "Ariel," a name occurring in the Bible (Isaiah xxix, 1), was among them.

The imagery of contemporary accounts of Atlantic voyages has also left strong traces in *The Tempest*, and seems almost to have been its immediate inspiration. One ship of a fleet that sailed across the ocean to reinforce Ralegh's Virginian colony in 1609 had an experience rather like that of Alonso's ship. It was driven aground on the Bermudas by a storm and given up for lost, but the passengers managed to survive the winter there and reached Virginia the following spring. William Strachey's account of this experience, *True Repertory of the Wracke*, dated July 15, 1610, was not published until after Shakespeare's death, and as Shakespeare certainly knew it, he must have read it in manuscript. Strachey's and a closely related pamphlet, Sylvester Jourdain's *Discovery of the Barmudas* (1610), lie behind Caliban's allusions to making dams for fish and to water with "berries" (i.e. cedar-berries) in it. Other details indicate Shakespeare's reading in similar accounts. Setebos is mentioned as a god ("divell") of the Patagonians in Richard Eden's *History of Travayle in the West and East Indies* (1577), and the curious "Bowgh, wawgh" refrain in Ariel's first song seems to be from a contemporary account of an Indian dance. It is a little puzzling why New World imagery should be so prominent in *The Tempest*, which really has nothing to do with the New World, beyond Ariel's reference to the "still-vexed Bermoothes" and a general, if vague, resemblance between the relation of Caliban to the other characters and that of the American Indians to the colonizers and drunken sailors who came to exterminate or enslave them.

However that may be, the dates of these pamphlets help to establish the fact that *The Tempest* is a very late play. A performance of it is recorded for November 1, 1611, in Whitehall, and it also formed part of the celebrations connected with the wedding of King James' daughter Elizabeth in the winter of 1612–13. The versification is also that of a late play, for *The Tempest* is written in the direct speaking style of Shakespeare's last period, the lines full of weak endings and so welded together that every speech is a verse paragraph in itself, often very close in its rhythm to prose, especially in the speeches of Caliban. One should read the verse as an actor would read it, attending to the natural stresses, of which there are usually four to a line, rather than the metre. Some critics have felt that a few lines are "unmetrical," but no line that can be easily spoken on the stage is unmetrical, and it is simple enough to find the four natural stresses in "You do *look*, my *son*, in a *moved sort*," or (in octosyllabics) "*Earth's in*crease, *foi*son *plen*ty." In such writing all the regular schematic forms of verse, rhyme, alliteration, assonance, and the like, fall into the background, peeping out irregularly through the texture:

> I will stand to, and feed;
> Although my last, no matter, since I feel
> The best is past. Brother, my lord the Duke,
> Stand to, and do as we.

In its genre *The Tempest* shows a marked affinity with dramatic forms outside the normal range of tragedy and comedy. Among these is the masque: besides containing an actual masque, *The Tempest* is like the masque in its use of elaborate stage machinery and music. The magician with his wand and mantle was a frequent figure in masques, and Caliban is like the "wild men" common in the farcical interludes known as antimasques. Another is the *commedia dell'arte*, which was well known in England. Some of the sketchy plots of this half-improvised type of play have been preserved, and they show extraordinary similarities to *The Tempest*, especially in the Stephano–Trinculo scenes. *The Tempest* in short is a spectacular and operatic play, and when we think of other plays like it, we are more apt to think of, say, Mozart's *Magic Flute* than of ordinary stage plays.

But more important than these affiliations is the position of *The Tempest* as the fourth and last of the great romances of Shakespeare's final period. In these plays Shakespeare seems to have distilled the essence of all his work in tragedy, comedy, and history, and to have reached the very bedrock of drama itself, with a romantic spectacle which is at once primitive and sophisticated, childlike and profound. In these plays the central structural principles of drama emerge with great clarity, and we become aware of the affinity between the happy endings of comedy and the rituals marking the great rising rhythms of life: marriage, springtime, harvest, dawn, and rebirth. In *The Tempest* there is also an emphasis on moral and spiritual rebirth which suggests rituals of initiation, like baptism or the ancient mystery dramas, as well as of festivity. And just as its poetic texture ranges from the simplicity of Ariel's incredibly beautiful songs to the haunting solemnity of Prospero's speeches, so we may come to the play on any level, as a fairy tale with unusually lifelike characters, or as an inexhaustibly profound drama that has influenced some of the most complex poems in the language, including Milton's *Comus* and Eliot's *The Waste Land*. However we take it, *The Tempest* is a play not simply to be read or seen or even studied, but possessed.

Victoria College   NORTHROP FRYE
University of Toronto

NOTE ON THE TEXT

The Tempest was first printed in the folio of 1623, evidently from a transcript (made by the scrivener Ralph Crane) of Shakespeare's draft after it had been prepared for production. The play stands first in the volume, in a carefully edited and printed text, supplied with unusually full stage directions, and a list of characters (following the Epilogue). The present edition follows the folio text; except for occasional relineation, departures from it are few and slight. The act–scene division supplied marginally is that of the folio. Below are listed all substantive departures from the folio text, with the adopted reading in italics followed by the folio reading in roman.

The Scene . . . Island followed by *Names of the Actors* (appears after Epilogue in F)

I, i, 31 *Exeunt* Exit   34 *plague* plague –   46–47 *courses! Off courses* off   56–58 *Mercy . . . split* (assigned to Gonzalo in F)   59 *with th' King* with' King

I, ii, 100 *unto* into   112 *with th' King* with King   145 *prepared* preparèd   159 *divine.* divine   201 *lightnings* Lightning   230 *stowed* stowèd   248 *made no* made thee no   271 *wast* was   282 *she* he   374 s.d. *Ariel's song* Ariel Song   380 *the burden bear* beare the burthen   381 *Hark, hark!* (appears after s.d. *Burthen dispersedly* in l. 379 in F)   384 s.d. *Burden, dispersedly* (not in F)   396 s.d. *Ariel's song* Ariell Song

II, i, 5 *master* Masters   36 *Ha, ha, ha!* (assigned to Sebastian in F)   37 *So, you're paid* (assigned to Antonio in F)   62 *gloss* glosses   90 *Ay* I   106 *removed* removèd   114 *oared* oarèd   116 *bowed* bowèd

II, ii, 45 (F has s.d. *Sings*)   173 *Caliban* (omitted in F)

III, i, 2 *sets* set   15 *least* lest   93 *withal* with all

III, ii, 14 *on, by this light. Thou* on, by this light thou   51–52 *isle; From me* Isle From me,   118 *scout* cout   149 *Wilt come?* (assigned to Trinculo in F)   150 *I'll follow, Stephano* Ile follow Stephano

III, iii, 2 *ache* akes   17 *Sebastian . . . more* (appears after s.d. *Solemne . . . depart* in F)   29 *islanders* Islands   65 *plume* plumbe

IV, i, 9 *off* of   13 *gift* guest   17 *rite* right   52 *rein* raigne   73 (F has s.d. *Iuno descends*)   74 *her* here   106 *marriage blessing* marriage, blessing   145 *anger so* anger, so   193 s.d. *Enter*

NOTE ON THE TEXT

Ariel . . . &c. (appears after *line* in F)   *them on* on them   230
Let't let's   262 *Lie* Lies
V, i, 16 *run* runs   60 *boiled* boile   72 *Didst* Did   75 *entertained*
entertaine   76 *who* whom   82 *lies* ly   124 *not* nor   136 *who*
whom   199 *remembrance* remembrances   236 *her* our   248
Which shall be shortly, single I'll (Which shall be shortly single)
I'le   258 *coragio* Corasio

THE TEMPEST

Alonso, King of Naples
Sebastian, his brother
Prospero, the right Duke of Milan
Antonio, his brother, the usurping Duke of Milan
Ferdinand, son to the King of Naples
Gonzalo, an honest old councillor
Adrian and Francisco, lords
Caliban, a savage and deformed slave
Trinculo, a jester
Stephano, a drunken butler
Master of a ship
Boatswain
Mariners
Miranda, daughter to Prospero
Ariel, an airy spirit
Iris
Ceres
Juno } *[presented by] spirits*
Nymphs
Reapers
[Other spirits attending on Prospero]

The Scene : *An uninhabited Island*

THE TEMPEST

A tempestuous noise of thunder and lightning heard.
Enter a Shipmaster and a Boatswain.

MASTER Boatswain!

BOATSWAIN Here, master. What cheer?

MASTER Good, speak to th' mariners; fall to't yarely, or 3
we run ourselves aground. Bestir, bestir! *Exit.*
Enter Mariners.

BOATSWAIN Heigh, my hearts! Cheerly, cheerly, my
hearts! Yare, yare! Take in the topsail! Tend to th' 6
master's whistle! Blow till thou burst thy wind, if room 7
enough!
Enter Alonso, Sebastian, Antonio, Ferdinand,
Gonzalo, and others.

ALONSO Good boatswain, have care. Where's the master? Play the men.   9

BOATSWAIN I pray now, keep below.

ANTONIO Where is the master, bos'n?

BOATSWAIN Do you not hear him? You mar our labor.
Keep your cabins: you do assist the storm.

GONZALO Nay, good, be patient.

BOATSWAIN When the sea is. Hence! What cares these
roarers for the name of king? To cabin! Silence! 15
Trouble us not!

I, i The deck of a ship   3 *yarely* briskly   6 *Tend* attend   7 *Blow . . . wind*
(addressed to the storm)   7–8 *if room enough* i.e. so long as we have sea-
room   9 *Play* (perhaps 'ply,' keep the men busy)   15 *roarers* (1) waves,
(2) blusterers or bullies

29

GONZALO Good, yet remember whom thou hast aboard.

BOATSWAIN None that I more love than myself. You are
a councillor: if you can command these elements to si-
21   lence and work the peace of the present, we will not hand
a rope more; use your authority. If you cannot, give
thanks you have lived so long, and make yourself ready
in your cabin for the mischance of the hour, if it so hap.
– Cheerly, good hearts! – Out of our way, I say.   *Exit.*

GONZALO I have great comfort from this fellow: me-
27   thinks he hath no drowning mark upon him; his com-
28   plexion is perfect gallows. Stand fast, good Fate, to his
hanging! Make the rope of his destiny our cable, for
30   our own doth little advantage. If he be not born to be
hanged, our case is miserable.   *Exeunt.*
        Enter Boatswain.

BOATSWAIN Down with the topmast! Yare! Lower,
33   lower! Bring her to try with main-course! *(A cry*
34   *within.)* A plague upon this howling! They are louder
35   than the weather or our office.
        Enter Sebastian, Antonio, and Gonzalo.
Yet again? What do you here? Shall we give o'er and
drown? Have you a mind to sink?

SEBASTIAN A pox o' your throat, you bawling, blas-
phemous, incharitable dog!

BOATSWAIN Work you, then.

ANTONIO Hang, cur, hang, you whoreson, insolent noise-
maker! We are less afraid to be drowned than thou art.

43   GONZALO I'll warrant him for drowning, though the ship

---

21 *hand* handle   27 *complexion* indication of character in appearance of
face   28 *gallows* (alluding to the proverb 'He that's born to be hanged need
fear no drowning')   30 *doth little advantage* doesn't help us much   33 *try
with main-course* lie hove-to with only the mainsail   34 *plague* (followed by a
dash in F; possibly the boatswain's language was more profane than the text
indicates; cf. l. 38, and V, i, 218–19)   35 *our office* (the noise we make at)
our work   43 *warrant . . . for* guarantee . . . against

were no stronger than a nutshell and as leaky as an
unstanched wench.   45

BOATSWAIN Lay her ahold, ahold! Set her two courses!   46
     Off to sea again! Lay her off!

       Enter Mariners wet.

MARINERS All lost! To prayers, to prayers! All lost!
                                       [Exeunt.]

BOATSWAIN What, must our mouths be cold?

GONZALO
     The King and Prince at prayers! Let's assist them,
     For our case is as theirs.

SEBASTIAN   I am out of patience.

ANTONIO
     We are merely cheated of our lives by drunkards.   52
     This wide-chopped rascal – would thou mightst lie   53
         drowning
     The washing of ten tides!   54

GONZALO   He'll be hanged yet,
     Though every drop of water swear against it
     And gape at wid'st to glut him.   56

       A confused noise within :
                         'Mercy on us! –
     We split, we split! – Farewell, my wife and children! –
     Farewell, brother! – We split, we split, we split!'
                           [Exit Boatswain.]

ANTONIO
     Let's all sink with th' King.

SEBASTIAN   Let's take leave of him.
                           Exit [with Antonio].

GONZALO Now would I give a thousand furlongs of sea

---

45 *unstanched* i.e. loose   46 *ahold* (perhaps 'a-hull,' without any sail. As the
ship drifts to the rocks, the order is reversed and the *two courses*, foresail and
mainsail, are set up again in an effort to clear the shore.)   52 *merely* com-
pletely   53 *wide-chopped* wide-jawed   54 *ten tides* (pirates were hanged on
shore and left until three tides washed over them)   56 *glut* gobble

61   for an acre of barren ground – long heath, brown furze,
     anything. The wills above be done, but I would fain die
     a dry death.   *Exit.*

                            ✳

I, ii   *Enter Prospero and Miranda.*

     MIRANDA
        If by your art, my dearest father, you have
        Put the wild waters in this roar, allay them.
        The sky, it seems, would pour down stinking pitch
4   But that the sea, mounting to th' welkin's cheek,
        Dashes the fire out. O, I have sufferèd
6   With those that I saw suffer! a brave vessel
        (Who had no doubt some noble creature in her)
        Dashed all to pieces! O, the cry did knock
        Against my very heart! Poor souls, they perished!
        Had I been any god of power, I would
11   Have sunk the sea within the earth or ere
        It should the good ship so have swallowed and
13   The fraughting souls within her.
     PROSPERO   Be collected.
14   No more amazement. Tell your piteous heart
        There's no harm done.
     MIRANDA   O, woe the day!
     PROSPERO   No harm.
        I have done nothing but in care of thee,
        Of thee my dear one, thee my daughter, who
        Art ignorant of what thou art, naught knowing
        Of whence I am; nor that I am more better
        Than Prospero, master of a full poor cell,
        And thy no greater father.

61 *long heath, brown furze* heather and gorse (sometimes emended to 'ling,
heath, broom, furze')
I, ii Before Prospero's cell   4 *cheek* face (with perhaps a secondary meaning of 'side of a grate')   6 *brave* fine, handsome (and so elsewhere through-
out the play)   11 *or ere* before   13 *fraughting* forming the cargo; *collected*
composed   14 *amazement* distraction; *piteous* pitying

MIRANDA   More to know
  Did never meddle with my thoughts.   22
PROSPERO   'Tis time
  I should inform thee farther. Lend thy hand
  And pluck my magic garment from me. So,
  Lie there, my art. Wipe thou thine eyes; have comfort.   25
  The direful spectacle of the wrack, which touched
  The very virtue of compassion in thee,   27
  I have with such provision in mine art   28
  So safely orderèd that there is no soul –
  No, not so much perdition as an hair   30
  Betid to any creature in the vessel   31
  Which thou heard'st cry, which thou saw'st sink. Sit
      down;
  For thou must now know farther.
MIRANDA   You have often
  Begun to tell me what I am; but stopped
  And left me to a bootless inquisition,   35
  Concluding, 'Stay : not yet.'
PROSPERO   The hour's now come;
  The very minute bids thee ope thine ear.
  Obey, and be attentive. Canst thou remember   38
  A time before we came unto this cell?
  I do not think thou canst, for then thou wast not
  Out three years old.   41
MIRANDA   Certainly, sir, I can.
PROSPERO
  By what? By any other house or person?
  Of any thing the image tell me that   43
  Hath kept with thy remembrance.
MIRANDA   'Tis far off,
  And rather like a dream than an assurance
  That my remembrance warrants. Had I not   46

22 meddle mingle   25 art i.e. his robe   27 virtue essence   28 provision fore-
sight   30 perdition loss   31 Betid happened   35 bootless inquisition fruitless
inquiry   38 Obey listen   41 Out fully   43 tell me i.e. describe for me   46
remembrance warrants memory guarantees

  Four or five women once that tended me ?

PROSPERO

  Thou hadst, and more, Miranda. But how is it
  That this lives in thy mind ? What seest thou else
50 In the dark backward and abysm of time ?
  If thou rememb'rest aught ere thou cam'st here,
  How thou cam'st here thou mayst.

MIRANDA   But that I do not.

PROSPERO

  Twelve year since, Miranda, twelve year since,
  Thy father was the Duke of Milan and
  A prince of power.

MIRANDA   Sir, are not you my father ?

PROSPERO

56 Thy mother was a piece of virtue, and
  She said thou wast my daughter ; and thy father
  Was Duke of Milan ; and his only heir
59 A princess – no worse issuèd.

MIRANDA   O the heavens !

  What foul play had we that we came from thence ?
  Or blessèd was't we did ?

PROSPERO   Both, both, my girl !

  By foul play, as thou say'st, were we heaved thence,
63 But blessedly holp hither.

MIRANDA   O, my heart bleeds

64 To think o' th' teen that I have turned you to,
65 Which is from my remembrance ! Please you, farther.

PROSPERO

  My brother and thy uncle, called Antonio –
  I pray thee mark me – that a brother should
  Be so perfidious ! – he whom next thyself
69 Of all the world I loved, and to him put

---

50 *backward* past; *abysm* abyss 56 *piece* masterpiece 59 *no worse issuèd* no
meaner in descent 63 *blessedly holp* providentially helped 64 *teen* trouble;
turned you to put you in mind of 65 *from* out of 69–70 *put . . . state* en-
trusted the control of my administration

The manage of my state, as at that time
Through all the signories it was the first   71
And Prospero the prime duke, being so reputed
In dignity, and for the liberal arts
Without a parallel; those being all my study,
The government I cast upon my brother
And to my state grew stranger, being transported
And rapt in secret studies. Thy false uncle –
Dost thou attend me?

MIRANDA   Sir, most heedfully.

PROSPERO

Being once perfected how to grant suits,   79
How to deny them, who t' advance, and who
To trash for over-topping, new-created   81
The creatures that were mine, I say, or changed 'em,   82
Or else new-formed 'em; having both the key   83
Of officer and office, set all hearts i' th' state
To what tune pleased his ear, that now he was
The ivy which had hid my princely trunk
And sucked my verdure out on't. Thou attend'st not?

MIRANDA

O, good sir, I do.

PROSPERO   I pray thee mark me.

I thus neglecting worldly ends, all dedicated
To closeness, and the bettering of my mind   90
With that which, but by being so retired,
O'er-prized all popular rate, in my false brother   92
Awaked an evil nature, and my trust,
Like a good parent, did beget of him   94
A falsehood in its contrary as great
As my trust was, which had indeed no limit,

---

71 *signories* states of northern Italy   79 *perfected* grown skillful   81 *trash for over-topping* (1) check, as hounds, for going too fast, (2) cut branches, as of over-tall trees   82 *or* either   83 *key* (used with pun on its musical sense, leading to the metaphor of *tune*)   90 *closeness* seclusion (?), secret studies (?)   92 *O'er-prized* outvalued; *rate* estimation   94 *good parent* (alluding to the same proverb cited by Miranda in l. 120)

97 A confidence sans bound. He being thus lorded,
98 Not only with what my revenue yielded
   But what my power might else exact, like one
100 Who having unto truth, by telling of it,
   Made such a sinner of his memory
102 To credit his own lie, he did believe
103 He was indeed the Duke, out o' th' substitution
   And executing th' outward face of royalty
   With all prerogative. Hence his ambition growing –
   Dost thou hear?

MIRANDA   Your tale, sir, would cure deafness.

PROSPERO
   To have no screen between this part he played
   And him he played it for, he needs will be
109 Absolute Milan. Me (poor man) my library
   Was dukedom large enough. Of temporal royalties
111 He thinks me now incapable; confederates
112 (So dry he was for sway) with th' King of Naples
   To give him annual tribute, do him homage,
   Subject his coronet to his crown, and bend
   The dukedom yet unbowed (alas, poor Milan!)
   To most ignoble stooping.

MIRANDA   O the heavens!

PROSPERO
117 Mark his condition, and th' event; then tell me
   If this might be a brother.

MIRANDA   I should sin
   To think but nobly of my grandmother.
   Good wombs have borne bad sons.

PROSPERO   Now the condition.
   This King of Naples, being an enemy
   To me inveterate, hearkens my brother's suit;

97–99 *He ... exact* (the sense is that Antonio had the prerogatives as well as
the income of the Duke) 97 *sans bound* unlimited 98 *revenue* (accent
second syllable) 100 *it* i.e. the lie 102 *To* as to 103 *out* as a result 109
Absolute Milan Duke of Milan in fact 111 *confederates* joins in league with
112 *dry* thirsty, eager 117 *condition* pact; *event* outcome

Which was, that he, in lieu o' th' premises   123
Of homage and I know not how much tribute,
Should presently extirpate me and mine   125
Out of the dukedom and confer fair Milan,
With all the honors, on my brother. Whereon,
A treacherous army levied, one midnight
Fated to th' purpose, did Antonio open   129
The gates of Milan; and i' th' dead of darkness,
The ministers for th' purpose hurrièd thence   131
Me and thy crying self.

MIRANDA   Alack, for pity!
I, not rememb'ring how I cried out then,
Will cry it o'er again; it is a hint   134
That wrings mine eyes to't.   135

PROSPERO   Hear a little further,
And then I'll bring thee to the present business
Which now's upon's; without the which this story
Were most impertinent.   138

MIRANDA   Wherefore did they not
That hour destroy us?

PROSPERO   Well demanded, wench.
My tale provokes that question. Dear, they durst not,
So dear the love my people bore me; nor set
A mark so bloody on the business; but
With colors fairer painted their foul ends.
In few, they hurried us aboard a bark,   144
Bore us some leagues to sea; where they prepared
A rotten carcass of a butt, not rigged,   146
Nor tackle, sail, nor mast; the very rats
Instinctively have quit it. There they hoist us,
To cry to th' sea that roared to us; to sigh
To th' winds, whose pity, sighing back again,
Did us but loving wrong.

---

123 *in lieu o' th' premises* in return for the guarantees   125 *presently* immediately; *extirpate* remove (accent second syllable)   129 *Fated* devoted
131 *ministers* agents   134 *hint* occasion   135 *wrings* constrains   138 *impertinent* irrelevant   144 *few* few words   146 *butt* tub

MIRANDA   Alack, what trouble
Was I then to you!

PROSPERO   O, a cherubin
Thou wast that did preserve me! Thou didst smile,
Infusèd with a fortitude from heaven,
When I have decked the sea with drops full salt,
Under my burden groaned: which raised in me
157   An undergoing stomach, to bear up
Against what should ensue.

MIRANDA   How came we ashore?

PROSPERO
By providence divine.
Some food we had, and some fresh water, that
A noble Neapolitan, Gonzalo,
Out of his charity, who being then appointed
Master of this design, did give us, with
Rich garments, linens, stuffs, and necessaries
165   Which since have steaded much. So, of his gentleness,
Knowing I loved my books, he furnished me
From mine own library with volumes that
I prize above my dukedom.

MIRANDA   Would I might
But ever see that man!

PROSPERO   Now I arise.
Sit still, and hear the last of our sea-sorrow.
Here in this island we arrived; and here
172   Have I, thy schoolmaster, made thee more profit
173   Than other princess can, that have more time
For vainer hours, and tutors not so careful.

MIRANDA
Heavens thank you for't! And now I pray you, sir, –
For still 'tis beating in my mind, – your reason
For raising this sea-storm?

PROSPERO   Know thus far forth.

---

157 *undergoing stomach* resolution to endure   **165** *steaded* been of use   **172**
more profit profit more   **173** *princess* princesses

By accident most strange, bountiful Fortune
(Now, my dear lady) hath mine enemies
Brought to this shore ; and by my prescience   *forsight*
I find my zenith doth depend upon   181
A most auspicious star, whose influence
If now I court not, but omit, my fortunes   183
Will ever after droop. Here cease more questions.
Thou art inclined to sleep. 'Tis a good dulness,
And give it way. I know thou canst not choose.
    [Miranda sleeps.]
Come away, servant, come ! I am ready now.   187
Approach, my Ariel : come !
    Enter Ariel.

ARIEL
All hail, great master ! Grave sir, hail ! I come
To answer thy best pleasure ; be't to fly,
To swim, to dive into the fire, to ride
On the curled clouds. To thy strong bidding task   192
Ariel and all his quality.   193
PROSPERO   Hast thou, spirit,
Performed to point the tempest that I bade thee ?   194
ARIEL
To every article.
I boarded the King's ship : now on the beak,   196
Now in the waist, the deck, in every cabin,   197
I flamed amazement : sometime I'ld divide   198
And burn in many places ; on the topmast,
The yards, and boresprit would I flame distinctly,   200
Then meet and join. Jove's lightnings, the precursors
O' th' dreadful thunderclaps, more momentary
And sight-outrunning were not. The fire and cracks
Of sulphurous roaring the most mighty Neptune

---

181 *zenith* apex of fortune   183 *omit* neglect   187 *Come away* come here
192 *task* (supply 'come')   193 *quality* cohorts (Ariel is leader of a band of
elemental spirits)   194 *to point* in detail   196 *beak* prow   197 *waist*
middle; *deck* poop   198 *flamed amazement* struck terror by appearing as
(St Elmo's) fire   200 *boresprit* bowsprit; *distinctly* in different places

Seem to besiege and make his bold waves tremble;
Yea, his dread trident shake.

PROSPERO   My brave spirit!
207   Who was so firm, so constant, that this coil
Would not infect his reason?

ARIEL   Not a soul
209   But felt a fever of the mad and played
Some tricks of desperation. All but mariners
Plunged in the foaming brine and quit the vessel;
212   Then all afire with me the King's son Ferdinand,
213   With hair up-staring (then like reeds, not hair),
Was the first man that leapt; cried 'Hell is empty,
And all the devils are here!'

PROSPERO   Why, that's my spirit!
But was not this nigh shore?

ARIEL   Close by, my master.

PROSPERO
But are they, Ariel, safe?

ARIEL   Not a hair perished.
218   On their sustaining garments not a blemish,
But fresher than before; and as thou bad'st me,
In troops I have dispersed them 'bout the isle.
The King's son have I landed by himself,
Whom I left cooling of the air with sighs
In an odd angle of the isle, and sitting,
224   His arms in this sad knot.

PROSPERO   Of the King's ship
The mariners say how thou hast disposed,
And all the rest o' th' fleet.

ARIEL   Safely in harbor
Is the King's ship; in the deep nook where once
Thou call'dst me up at midnight to fetch dew

---

207 *coil* uproar   209 *of the mad* such as madmen have   212 *afire with me*
(refers either to the vessel or to Ferdinand, depending on the punctuation;
F suggests the latter)   213 *up-staring* standing on end   218 *sustaining*
buoying them up in the water   224 *this* (illustrated by a gesture)

From the still-vexed Bermoothes, there she's hid;   229
The mariners all under hatches stowed,
Who, with a charm joined to their suff'red labor,   231
I have left asleep; and for the rest o' th' fleet,
Which I dispersed, they all have met again,
And are upon the Mediterranean flote   234
Bound sadly home for Naples,
Supposing that they saw the King's ship wracked
And his great person perish.

PROSPERO   Ariel, thy charge
Exactly is performed; but there's more work.
What is the time o' th' day?

ARIEL   Past the mid season.   239

PROSPERO
At least two glasses. The time 'twixt six and now   240
Must by us both be spent most preciously.

ARIEL
Is there more toil? Since thou dost give me pains,
Let me remember thee what thou hast promised,   243
Which is not yet performed me.

PROSPERO   How now? moody?
What is't thou canst demand?

ARIEL   My liberty.

PROSPERO
Before the time be out? No more!   246

ARIEL   I prithee,
Remember I have done thee worthy service,
Told thee no lies, made no mistakings, served
Without or grudge or grumblings. Thou did promise
To bate me a full year.   250

PROSPERO   Dost thou forget
From what a torment I did free thee?

ARIEL   No.

---

229 *still-vexed Bermoothes* constantly agitated Bermudas **231** *suff'red*
undergone **234** *flote* sea **239** *mid season* noon **240** *glasses* hours **243** *remember* remind **246** *time* period of service **250** *bate me* shorten my term
of service

PROSPERO
>   Thou dost ; and think'st it much to tread the ooze
>   Of the salt deep,
>   To run upon the sharp wind of the North,
255   To do me business in the veins o' th' earth
256   When it is baked with frost.

ARIEL   I do not, sir.

PROSPERO
>   Thou liest, malignant thing ! Hast thou forgot
258   The foul witch Sycorax, who with age and envy
>   Was grown into a hoop ? Hast thou forgot her ?

ARIEL
>   No, sir.

PROSPERO Thou hast. Where was she born ? Speak !
>   Tell me !

ARIEL
261   Sir, in Argier.

PROSPERO   O, was she so ? I must
>   Once in a month recount what thou hast been,
>   Which thou forget'st. This damned witch Sycorax,
>   For mischiefs manifold, and sorceries terrible
>   To enter human hearing, from Argier,
266   Thou know'st, was banished. For one thing she did
>   They would not take her life. Is not this true ?

ARIEL
>   Ay, sir.

PROSPERO
>   This blue-eyed hag was hither brought with child
>   And here was left by th' sailors. Thou, my slave,
>   As thou report'st thyself, wast then her servant ;
>   And, for thou wast a spirit too delicate
>   To act her earthy and abhorred commands,

---

255 *veins* streams   **256** *baked* hardened   **258** *Sycorax* (name not found elsewhere; usually connected with Greek '*sys*', sow, and '*korax*', which means both raven – cf. l. 322 – and curved, hence perhaps *hoop*); *envy* malice   **261** *Argier* Algiers   **266** *one thing she did* (being pregnant, her sentence was commuted from death to exile)

42

Refusing her grand hests, she did confine thee,   274
By help of her more potent ministers,
And in her most unmitigable rage,
Into a cloven pine ; within which rift
Imprisoned thou didst painfully remain
A dozen years ; within which space she died
And left thee there, where thou didst vent thy groans
As fast as millwheels strike. Then was this island   281
(Save for the son that she did litter here,
A freckled whelp, hag-born) not honored with
A human shape.

ARIEL   Yes, Caliban her son.

PROSPERO
Dull thing, I say so : he, that Caliban
Whom now I keep in service. Thou best know'st
What torment I did find thee in : thy groans
Did make wolves howl and penetrate the breasts
Of ever-angry bears. It was a torment
To lay upon the damned, which Sycorax
Could not again undo. It was mine art,
When I arrived and heard thee, that made gape
The pine, and let thee out.

ARIEL   I thank thee, master.

PROSPERO
If thou more murmur'st, I will rend an oak
And peg thee in his knotty entrails till   295
Thou hast howled away twelve winters.   296

ARIEL   Pardon, master.
I will be correspondent to command   297
And do my spriting gently.   298

PROSPERO   Do so ; and after two days
I will discharge thee.

ARIEL   That's my noble master !

274 *hests* commands   281 *millwheels* i.e. the clappers on the millwheels
295 *his* its   296 *twelve* (the same length of time that Ariel has been re-
leased)   297 *correspondent* obedient   298 *spriting gently* office as a spirit
graciously

What shall I do? Say what? What shall I do?

PROSPERO

Go make thyself like a nymph o' th' sea. Be subject
To no sight but thine and mine; invisible
To every eyeball else. Go take this shape
And hither come in't. Go! Hence with diligence!

                                        Exit [Ariel].

Awake, dear heart, awake! Thou hast slept well.
Awake!

MIRANDA The strangeness of your story put
Heaviness in me.

PROSPERO   Shake it off. Come on.
We'll visit Caliban, my slave, who never
Yields us kind answer.

MIRANDA   'Tis a villain, sir,
I do not love to look on.

PROSPERO   But as 'tis,

311   We cannot miss him: he does make our fire,
Fetch in our wood, and serves in offices
That profit us. What, ho! slave! Caliban!
Thou earth, thou! Speak!

CALIBAN *[within]*   There's wood enough within.

PROSPERO

Come forth, I say! There's other business for thee.

316   Come, thou tortoise! When?

                Enter Ariel like a water nymph.

317   Fine apparition! My quaint Ariel,
Hark in thine ear.

ARIEL   My lord, it shall be done.   *Exit.*

PROSPERO

Thou poisonous slave, got by the devil himself
Upon thy wicked dam, come forth!

                Enter Caliban.

CALIBAN

As wicked dew as e'er my mother brushed

311 *miss* do without   316 *When* (expression of impatience)   317 *quaint*
ingenious

With raven's feather from unwholesome fen
Drop on you both ! A south-west blow on ye
And blister you all o'er !

PROSPERO

For this, be sure, to-night thou shalt have cramps,
Side-stitches that shall pen thy breath up ; urchins   326
Shall, for that vast of night that they may work,   327
All exercise on thee ; thou shalt be pinched
As thick as honeycomb, each pinch more stinging
Than bees that made 'em.

CALIBAN   I must eat my dinner.

This island's mine by Sycorax my mother,
Which thou tak'st from me. When thou cam'st first,
Thou strok'st me and made much of me ; wouldst give me
Water with berries in't ; and teach me how
To name the bigger light, and how the less,
That burn by day and night ; and then I loved thee
And showed thee all the qualities o' th' isle,   337
The fresh springs, brine-pits, barren place and fertile.
Cursed be I that did so ! All the charms
Of Sycorax – toads, beetles, bats, light on you !
For I am all the subjects that you have,
Which first was mine own king ; and here you sty me
In this hard rock, whiles you do keep from me
The rest o' th' island.

PROSPERO   Thou most lying slave,
Whom stripes may move, not kindness ! I have used thee   345
(Filth as thou art) with humane care, and lodged thee
In mine own cell till thou didst seek to violate
The honor of my child.

CALIBAN

O ho, O ho ! Would't had been done !
Thou didst prevent me ; I had peopled else
This isle with Calibans.

326 *urchins* hedgehogs (i.e. goblins in that shape) 327 *vast* void; *that they
may work* (referring to the belief that malignant spirits had power only
during darkness) 337 *qualities* resources 345 *stripes* lashes

351 MIRANDA   Abhorrèd slave,
   Which any print of goodness wilt not take,
   Being capable of all ill ! I pitied thee,
   Took pains to make thee speak, taught thee each hour
   One thing or other : when thou didst not, savage,
   Know thine own meaning, but wouldst gabble like
357 A thing most brutish, I endowed thy purposes
358 With words that made them known. But thy vile race,
359 Though thou didst learn, had that in't which good
     natures
   Could not abide to be with ; therefore wast thou
   Deservedly confined into this rock, who hadst
   Deserved more than a prison.

CALIBAN
   You taught me language, and my profit on't
364 Is, I know how to curse. The red plague rid you
   For learning me your language !

PROSPERO   Hag-seed, hence !
366 Fetch us in fuel ; and be quick, thou'rt best,
   To answer other business. Shrug'st thou, malice ?
   If thou neglect'st or dost unwillingly
369 What I command, I'll rack thee with old cramps,
370 Fill all thy bones with aches, make thee roar
   That beasts shall tremble at thy din.

CALIBAN   No, pray thee.
   [Aside]
   I must obey. His art is of such pow'r
   It would control my dam's god, Setebos,
   And make a vassal of him.

PROSPERO   So, slave ; hence !
             Exit Caliban.

351 *Miranda* (so F; some editors have given the speech to Prospero) 357
purposes meanings 358 *race* nature 359 *good natures* natural virtues 364
red plague bubonic plague; *rid* destroy 366 *thou'rt best* you'd be well
advised 369 *old* i.e. such as old people have 370 *aches* (pronounced
'aitches')

Enter Ferdinand ; and Ariel (invisible), playing and singing.

Ariel's song.

> Come unto these yellow sands,
> > And then take hands.
> Curtsied when you have and kissed,
> > The wild waves whist, —calm down 378
> Foot it featly here and there ; 379
> And, sweet sprites, the burden bear. 380
> > Hark, hark !
> *Burden, dispersedly* Bowgh, wawgh !
> > The watchdogs bark.
> *Burden, dispersedly* Bowgh, wawgh !
> > Hark, hark ! I hear
> The strain of strutting chanticleer roosters
> > Cry cock-a-diddle-dowe. (a farm)

silly different directions

FERDINAND
Where should this music be ? I' th' air or th' earth ?
It sounds no more ; and sure it waits upon
Some god o' th' island. Sitting on a bank,
Weeping again the King my father's wrack,
This music crept by me upon the waters,
Allaying both their fury and my passion 393
With its sweet air. Thence I have followed it,
Or it hath drawn me rather ; but 'tis gone.
No, it begins again.

Ariel's song.

> Full fathom five thy father lies ;
> > Of his bones are coral made ;
> Those are pearls that were his eyes ;
> > Nothing of him that doth fade

---

378 *whist* being hushed   379 *featly* nimbly   380 *burden* undersong, refrain
393 *passion* lamentation

But doth suffer a sea-change
Into something rich and strange.
Sea nymphs hourly ring his knell :
Burden.   Ding-dong.
Hark ! now I hear them – Ding-dong bell.

FERDINAND

406 The ditty does remember my drowned father.
This is no mortal business, nor no sound
408 That the earth owes. I hear it now above me.

PROSPERO

409 The fringèd curtains of thine eye advance
And say what thou seest yond.

MIRANDA   What is't ? a spirit ?
Lord, how it looks about ! Believe me, sir,
It carries a brave form. But 'tis a spirit.

PROSPERO

No, wench : it eats, and sleeps, and hath such senses
As we have, such. This gallant which thou seest
415 Was in the wrack ; and, but he's something stained
With grief (that's beauty's canker), thou mightst call him
A goodly person. He hath lost his fellows
And strays about to find 'em.

MIRANDA   I might call him
A thing divine ; for nothing natural
I ever saw so noble.

PROSPERO *[aside]*   It goes on, I see,
421 As my soul prompts it. Spirit, fine spirit, I'll free thee
Within two days for this.

422 FERDINAND   Most sure, the goddess
On whom these airs attend ! Vouchsafe my prayer
424 May know if you remain upon this island,
And that you will some good instruction give
426 How I may bear me here. My prime request,

---

406 *remember* allude to   408 *owes* owns   409 *advance* raise   415 *stained*
disfigured   421 *prompts* would like   422 *Most sure* this is certainly   424
remain dwell   426 *bear me* conduct myself

Which I do last pronounce, is (O you wonder!)
If you be maid or no?

MIRANDA   No wonder, sir,
But certainly a maid.

FERDINAND   My language? Heavens!
I am the best of them that speak this speech,
Were I but where 'tis spoken.

PROSPERO   How? the best?
What wert thou if the King of Naples heard thee?

FERDINAND
A single thing, as I am now, that wonders   433
To hear thee speak of Naples. He does hear me;
And that he does I weep. Myself am Naples,   435
Who with mine eyes, never since at ebb, beheld
The King my father wracked.

MIRANDA   Alack, for mercy!

FERDINAND
Yes, faith, and all his lords, the Duke of Milan
And his brave son being twain.   439

PROSPERO [aside]   The Duke of Milan
And his more braver daughter could control thee,   440
If now 'twere fit to do't. At the first sight
They have changed eyes. Delicate Ariel,   442
I'll set thee free for this. – A word, good sir.
I fear you have done yourself some wrong. A word!   444

MIRANDA
Why speaks my father so ungently? This
Is the third man that e'er I saw; the first
That e'er I sighed for. Pity move my father
To be inclined my way!

FERDINAND   O, if a virgin,
And your affection not gone forth, I'll make you
The Queen of Naples.

---

433 *single* (1) solitary, (2) weak or helpless   435 *Naples* King of Naples
439 *son* (Antonio's son is not elsewhere mentioned)   440 *control* refute
442 *changed eyes* exchanged love looks   444 *done . . . wrong* told a lie

PROSPERO   Soft, sir! one word more.
              [Aside]
     They are both in either's pow'rs. But this swift business
     I must uneasy make, lest too light winning
     Make the prize light. – One word more! I charge thee
     That thou attend me. Thou dost here usurp
455 The name thou ow'st not, and hast put thyself
     Upon this island as a spy, to win it
     From me, the lord on't.

FERDINAND   No, as I am a man!

MIRANDA
     There's nothing ill can dwell in such a temple.
     If the ill spirit have so fair a house,
     Good things will strive to dwell with't.

PROSPERO   Follow me. –
     Speak not you for him; he's a traitor. – Come!
     I'll manacle thy neck and feet together;
     Sea water shalt thou drink; thy food shall be
     The fresh-brook mussels, withered roots, and husks
     Wherein the acorn cradled. Follow!

FERDINAND   No.
466 I will resist such entertainment till
     Mine enemy has more pow'r.
              He draws, and is charmed from moving.

MIRANDA   O dear father,
468 Make not too rash a trial of him, for
469 He's gentle, and not fearful.

PROSPERO   What, I say,
470 My foot my tutor? – Put thy sword up, traitor!
     Who mak'st a show but dar'st not strike, thy conscience
472 Is so possessed with guilt. Come, from thy ward!
     For I can here disarm thee with this stick
     And make thy weapon drop.

---

455 *ow'st* ownest   466 *entertainment* treatment   468 *trial* judgment   469
gentle noble; *fearful* cowardly   470 *My . . . tutor* i.e. instructed by my
underling   472 *ward* fighting posture

MIRANDA   Beseech you, father!
PROSPERO
   Hence! Hang not on my garments.
MIRANDA   Sir, have pity.
   I'll be his surety.
PROSPERO   Silence! One word more
   Shall make me chide thee, if not hate thee. What,
   An advocate for an impostor? Hush!
   Thou think'st there is no more such shapes as he,
   Having seen but him and Caliban. Foolish wench!
   To th' most of men this is a Caliban,
   And they to him are angels.
MIRANDA   My affections   482
   Are then most humble. I have no ambition
   To see a goodlier man.
PROSPERO   Come on, obey!   484
   Thy nerves are in their infancy again   485
   And have no vigor in them.
FERDINAND   So they are.
   My spirits, as in a dream, are all bound up.
   My father's loss, the weakness which I feel,
   The wrack of all my friends, nor this man's threats
   To whom I am subdued, are but light to me,
   Might I but through my prison once a day
   Behold this maid. All corners else o' th' earth
   Let liberty make use of. Space enough
   Have I in such a prison.
PROSPERO *[aside]*   It works. *[to Ferdinand]* Come on. –
   Thou hast done well, fine Ariel!
      [To Ferdinand]   Follow me.
      [To Ariel]
   Hark what thou else shalt do me.
MIRANDA   Be of comfort.
   My father's of a better nature, sir,
   Than he appears by speech. This is unwonted

482 *affections* inclinations   484 *obey* follow   485 *nerves* sinews, tendons

    Which now came from him.

PROSPERO   Thou shalt be as free

500   As mountain winds; but then exactly do
    All points of my command.

ARIEL   To th' syllable.

PROSPERO
    Come, follow. – Speak not for him.   *Exeunt.*

*

II, i   *Enter Alonso, Sebastian, Antonio, Gonzalo, Adrian,*
    Francisco, and others.

GONZALO
    Beseech you, sir, be merry. You have cause
    (So have we all) of joy; for our escape

3   Is much beyond our loss. Our hint of woe
    Is common: every day some sailor's wife,

5   The master of some merchant, and the merchant,
    Have just our theme of woe; but for the miracle,
    I mean our preservation, few in millions
    Can speak like us. Then wisely, good sir, weigh
    Our sorrow with our comfort.

ALONSO   Prithee peace.

10 SEBASTIAN He receives comfort like cold porridge.

11 ANTONIO The visitor will not give him o'er so.

SEBASTIAN Look, he's winding up the watch of his wit;
    by and by it will strike.

GONZALO Sir –

15 SEBASTIAN One. Tell.

GONZALO

16   When every grief is entertained, that's offered

---

500 *then* till then
II, i Another part of the island   **3** *hint* occasion   **5** *master of some merchant*
master of a merchant ship; *the merchant* the owner of the ship   **10** *porridge*
(pun on *peace* [pease])   **11** *visitor* spiritual adviser; *give him o'er* let him
alone   **15** *Tell* count   **16** *that's* that which is

Comes to th' entertainer –   17
SEBASTIAN A dollar.
GONZALO Dolor comes to him, indeed. You have spoken 19
    truer than you purposed.
SEBASTIAN You have taken it wiselier than I meant you
    should.
GONZALO Therefore, my lord –
ANTONIO Fie, what a spendthrift is he of his tongue!   24
ALONSO I prithee spare.
GONZALO Well, I have done. But yet –
SEBASTIAN He will be talking.
ANTONIO Which, of he or Adrian, for a good wager, first
    begins to crow?
SEBASTIAN The old cock.   30
ANTONIO The cock'rel.   31
SEBASTIAN Done! The wager?
ANTONIO A laughter.   33
SEBASTIAN A match!
ADRIAN Though this island seem to be desert –
ANTONIO Ha, ha, ha!
SEBASTIAN So, you're paid.
ADRIAN Uninhabitable and almost inaccessible –
SEBASTIAN Yet –
ADRIAN Yet –
ANTONIO He could not miss't.
ADRIAN It must needs be of subtle, tender, and delicate
    temperance.   43
ANTONIO Temperance was a delicate wench.   44
SEBASTIAN Ay, and a subtle, as he most learnedly de-
    livered.
ADRIAN The air breathes upon us here most sweetly.
SEBASTIAN As if it had lungs, and rotten ones.

---

17 *entertainer* (taken by Sebastian to mean 'innkeeper')   19 *Dolor* grief
(with pun on *dollar*, a continental coin)   24 *spendthrift* (Antonio labors the
pun)   30 *old cock* i.e. Gonzalo   31 *cock'rel* i.e. Adrian   33 *laughter* the
winner laughs   43 *temperance* climate   44 *Temperance* (a girl's name)

ANTONIO Or as 'twere perfumed by a fen.

GONZALO Here is everything advantageous to life.

ANTONIO True; save means to live.

SEBASTIAN Of that there's none, or little.

GONZALO How lush and lusty the grass looks! how green!

ANTONIO The ground indeed is tawny.

54 SEBASTIAN With an eye of green in't.

ANTONIO He misses not much.

SEBASTIAN No; he doth but mistake the truth totally.

GONZALO But the rarity of it is – which is indeed almost beyond credit –

59 SEBASTIAN As many vouched rarities are.

GONZALO That our garments, being, as they were, drenched in the sea, hold, notwithstanding, their freshness and gloss, being rather new-dyed than stained with salt water.

ANTONIO If but one of his pockets could speak, would it not say he lies?

SEBASTIAN Ay, or very falsely pocket up his report.

GONZALO Methinks our garments are now as fresh as when we put them on first in Afric, at the marriage of the King's fair daughter Claribel to the King of Tunis.

SEBASTIAN 'Twas a sweet marriage, and we prosper well in our return.

ADRIAN Tunis was never graced before with such a
72 paragon to their queen.

73 GONZALO Not since widow Dido's time.

ANTONIO Widow? A pox o' that! How came that 'widow' in? Widow Dido!

SEBASTIAN What if he had said 'widower Aeneas' too? Good Lord, how you take it!

---

54 *eye* spot (or perhaps Gonzalo's eye)   **59** *vouched rarities* wonders guaranteed to be true   **72** *to* for   **73** *widow Dido* (Dido was the widow of Sychaeus; Aeneas was a widower, having lost his wife in the fall of Troy. The reasons for Antonio's amusement, if that is what it is, have not been explained.)

ADRIAN 'Widow Dido,' said you? You make me study
   of that. She was of Carthage, not of Tunis.

GONZALO This Tunis, sir, was Carthage.

ADRIAN Carthage?

GONZALO I assure you, Carthage.

ANTONIO His word is more than the miraculous harp. 83

SEBASTIAN He hath raised the wall and houses too.

ANTONIO What impossible matter will he make easy
   next?

SEBASTIAN I think he will carry this island home in his
   pocket and give it his son for an apple.

ANTONIO And, sowing the kernels of it in the sea, bring
   forth more islands.

GONZALO Ay!   90

ANTONIO Why, in good time.

GONZALO Sir, we were talking that our garments seem
   now as fresh as when we were at Tunis at the marriage
   of your daughter, who is now Queen.

ANTONIO And the rarest that e'er came there.

SEBASTIAN Bate, I beseech you, widow Dido.   96

ANTONIO O, widow Dido? Ay, widow Dido!

GONZALO Is not, sir, my doublet as fresh as the first day I
   wore it? I mean, in a sort.   99

ANTONIO That 'sort' was well fished for.

GONZALO When I wore it at your daughter's marriage.

ALONSO
   You cram these words into mine ears against
   The stomach of my sense. Would I had never   103
   Married my daughter there! for, coming thence,
   My son is lost; and, in my rate, she too,   105
   Who is so far from Italy removed
   I ne'er again shall see her. O thou mine heir

---

83 *miraculous harp* (of Amphion, which raised the walls of Thebes; Tunis
and Carthage were near each other, but not the same city)   90 *Ay* (F reads
'I'; this and Antonio's rejoinder have not been satisfactorily explained)   96
Bate except   99 *in a sort* i.e. comparatively   103 *stomach . . . sense* i.e.
inclination of my mind   105 *rate* opinion

Of Naples and of Milan, what strange fish
Hath made his meal on thee? *death*

FRANCISCO   Sir, he may live.
I saw him beat the surges under him
And ride upon their backs. He trod the water,
Whose enmity he flung aside, and breasted
The surge most swol'n that met him. His bold head
'Bove the contentious waves he kept, and oared
Himself with his good arms in lusty stroke
116 To th' shore, that o'er his wave-worn basis bowed,
As stooping to relieve him. I not doubt
He came alive to land.

ALONSO   No, no, he's gone.

SEBASTIAN
Sir, you may thank yourself for this great loss,
That would not bless our Europe with your daughter,
But rather loose her to an African,
Where she, at least, is banished from your eye
Who hath cause to wet the grief on't.

ALONSO   Prithee peace.

SEBASTIAN
You were kneeled to and importuned otherwise
125 By all of us ; and the fair soul herself
Weighed, between loathness and obedience, at
Which end o` th' beam should bow. We have lost your
        son,
I fear, for ever. Milan and Naples have
129 Moe widows in them of this business' making
Than we bring men to comfort them :
The fault 's your own.

131 ALONSO   So is the dear'st o' th' loss.

GONZALO
My Lord Sebastian,
The truth you speak doth lack some gentleness,

116 *his* its; *basis* i.e. the sand   125–27 *the fair . . . bow* (the sense is that
Claribel hated the marriage, and only obedience to her father turned the
scale)   129 *Moe* more   131 *dear'st* heaviest

And time to speak it in. You rub the sore
When you should bring the plaster.

SEBASTIAN   Very well.

ANTONIO
And most chirurgeonly.   136

GONZALO
It is foul weather in us all, good sir,
When you are cloudy.

SEBASTIAN   Foul weather?

ANTONIO   Very foul.

GONZALO
Had I plantation of this isle, my lord –   139

ANTONIO
He'd sow't with nettle seed.

SEBASTIAN   Or docks, or mallows.

GONZALO
And were the king on't, what would I do?

SEBASTIAN
Scape being drunk for want of wine.

GONZALO
I' th' commonwealth I would by contraries   143
Execute all things; for no kind of traffic   144
Would I admit; no name of magistrate;   *no laws*
Letters should not be known; riches, poverty,
And use of service, none; contract, succession,   147
Bourn, bound of land, tilth, vineyard, none; *boundries* 148
No use of metal, corn, or wine, or oil;
No occupation; all men idle, all;
And women too, but innocent and pure;
No sovereignty.

SEBASTIAN   Yet he would be king on't.

ANTONIO The latter end of his commonwealth forgets
the beginning.

---

136 *chirurgeonly* like a surgeon 139 *plantation* colonization (taken by
Antonio in its other sense) 143 *by contraries* in contrast to usual customs
144 *traffic* trade 147 *use of service* having a servant class; *succession*
inheritance 148 *Bourn* limits of private property

GONZALO

All things in common nature should produce
Without sweat or endeavor. Treason, felony,
157   Sword, pike, knife, gun, or need of any engine
Would I not have ; but nature should bring forth,
159   Of it own kind, all foison, all abundance,
To feed my innocent people.

SEBASTIAN No marrying 'mong his subjects?

ANTONIO None, man, all idle – whores and knaves.

GONZALO

I would with such perfection govern, sir,
T' excel the golden age.

SEBASTIAN   Save his Majesty!

ANTONIO

Long live Gonzalo!

GONZALO   And – do you mark me, sir?

ALONSO

Prithee no more. Thou dost talk nothing to me.

GONZALO I do well believe your Highness ; and did it to
168   minister occasion to these gentlemen, who are of such
169   sensible and nimble lungs that they always use to laugh
at nothing.

ANTONIO 'Twas you we laughed at.

GONZALO Who in this kind of merry fooling am nothing
to you : so you may continue, and laugh at nothing still.

ANTONIO What a blow was there given!

175   SEBASTIAN An it had not fall'n flatlong.

GONZALO You are gentlemen of brave mettle; you
would lift the moon out of her sphere if she would continue in it five weeks without changing.

Enter Ariel, [invisible,] playing solemn music.

179   SEBASTIAN We would so, and then go a-batfowling.

ANTONIO Nay, good my lord, be not angry.

---

157 *engine* weapon **159** *it* its; *foison* abundance **168** *minister occasion*
afford opportunity **169** *sensible* sensitive **175** *An* if; *flatlong* struck with
the flat of a sword **179** *a-batfowling* hunting birds with sticks ('bats') at
night (using the moon for a lantern)

GONZALO No, I warrant you: I will not adventure my 181
   discretion so weakly. Will you laugh me asleep, for I am
   very heavy?
ANTONIO Go sleep, and hear us.
      [All sleep except Alonso, Sebastian, and Antonio.]
ALONSO
   What, all so soon asleep? I wish mine eyes
   Would, with themselves, shut up my thoughts. I find
   They are inclined to do so.
SEBASTIAN   Please you, sir,
   Do not omit the heavy offer of it.   188
   It seldom visits sorrow; when it doth,
   It is a comforter.
ANTONIO   We two, my lord,
   Will guard your person while you take your rest,
   And watch your safety.
ALONSO   Thank you. Wondrous heavy.
                    [Alonso sleeps. Exit Ariel.]

SEBASTIAN
   What a strange drowsiness possesses them!
ANTONIO
   It is the quality o' th' climate.
SEBASTIAN   Why
   Doth it not then our eyelids sink? I find not
   Myself disposed to sleep.
ANTONIO   Nor I: my spirits are nimble.
   They fell together all, as by consent.
   They dropped as by a thunder-stroke. What might,
   Worthy Sebastian – O, what might? – No more!
   And yet methinks I see it in thy face,
   What thou shouldst be. Th' occasion speaks thee, and   201
   My strong imagination sees a crown
   Dropping upon thy head.
SEBASTIAN   What? Art thou waking?

181 *adventure* risk (Gonzalo is saying, very politely, that their wit is too
feeble for him to take offense at it) 188 *omit* neglect; *heavy offer* opportunity its heaviness affords 201 *speaks* speaks to, summons

ANTONIO
Do you not hear me speak?

SEBASTIAN   I do; and surely
It is a sleepy language, and thou speak'st
Out of thy sleep. What is it thou didst say?
This is a strange repose, to be asleep
With eyes wide open; standing, speaking, moving,
And yet so fast asleep.

ANTONIO   Noble Sebastian,
210   Thou let'st thy fortune sleep – die, rather; wink'st
Whiles thou art waking.

SEBASTIAN   Thou dost snore distinctly;
There's meaning in thy snores.

ANTONIO
I am more serious than my custom. You
Must be so too, if heed me; which to do
215   Trebles thee o'er.

SEBASTIAN   Well, I am standing water.

ANTONIO
I'll teach you how to flow.

SEBASTIAN   Do so. To ebb
217   Hereditary sloth instructs me.

ANTONIO   O,
218   If you but knew how you the purpose cherish
Whiles thus you mock it! how, in stripping it,
220   You more invest it! Ebbing men indeed
(Most often) do so near the bottom run
By their own fear or sloth.

SEBASTIAN   Prithee say on.
The setting of thine eye and cheek proclaim
A matter from thee; and a birth, indeed,
225   Which throes thee much to yield.

ANTONIO   Thus, sir:

---

210 *wink'st* dost sleep   **215** *Trebles thee o'er* increases thy status threefold; *standing water* at slack tide   **217** *Hereditary sloth* natural laziness   **218** *cherish* enrich   **220** *invest* clothe   **225** *throes thee much* costs thee much pain, like a birth

Although this lord of weak remembrance, this 226
Who shall be of as little memory 227
When he is earthed, hath here almost persuaded 228
(For he's a spirit of persuasion, only
Professes to persuade) the King his son 's alive, 230
'Tis as impossible that he's undrowned
As he that sleeps here swims.
SEBASTIAN   I have no hope
That he's undrowned.
ANTONIO   O, out of that no hope
What great hope have you ! No hope that way is
Another way so high a hope that even
Ambition cannot pierce a wink beyond, 236
But doubt discovery there. Will you grant with me 237
That Ferdinand is drowned ?
SEBASTIAN   He's gone.
ANTONIO   Then tell me,
Who's the next heir of Naples ?
SEBASTIAN   Claribel.
ANTONIO
She that is Queen of Tunis ; she that dwells
Ten leagues beyond man's life ; she that from Naples 241
Can have no note, unless the sun were post – 242
The man i' th' moon 's too slow – till new-born chins
Be rough and razorable ; she that from whom
We all were sea-swallowed, though some cast again, 245
And, by that destiny, to perform an act
Whereof what's past is prologue, what to come,
In yours and my discharge. 248
SEBASTIAN   What stuff is this ? How say you ?
'Tis true my brother's daughter 's Queen of Tunis ;

226 *remembrance* memory 227 *of . . . memory* as little remembered 228
earthed buried 230 *Professes* has the function 236 *wink* glimpse 237
doubt discovery there is uncertain of seeing accurately 241 *Ten . . . life* i.e.
thirty miles from nowhere 242 *note* communication; *post* messenger 245
cast thrown up (with a suggestion of its theatrical meaning which introduces
the next metaphor) 248 *discharge* business

So is she heir of Naples; 'twixt which regions
There is some space.

ANTONIO   A space whose ev'ry cubit
Seems to cry out 'How shall that Claribel
253   Measure us back to Naples? Keep in Tunis,
And let Sebastian wake!' Say this were death
That now hath seized them, why, they were no worse
Than now they are. There be that can rule Naples
As well as he that sleeps; lords that can prate
As amply and unnecessarily
As this Gonzalo; I myself could make
260   A chough of as deep chat. O, that you bore
The mind that I do! What a sleep were this
For your advancement! Do you understand me?

SEBASTIAN
Methinks I do.

263 ANTONIO   And how does your content
Tender your own good fortune?

SEBASTIAN   I remember
You did supplant your brother Prospero.

ANTONIO   True.
And look how well my garments sit upon me,
267   Much feater than before. My brother's servants
268   Were then my fellows; now they are my men.

SEBASTIAN
But, for your conscience –

ANTONIO
270   Ay, sir, where lies that? If 'twere a kibe,
271   'Twould put me to my slipper; but I feel not
This deity in my bosom. Twenty consciences
273   That stand 'twixt me and Milan, candied be they
And melt, ere they molest! Here lies your brother,

no Consious

253 *us* i.e. the cubits   260 *chough* jackdaw (a bird sometimes taught to speak)   263–64 *content Tender* inclination estimate   267 *feater* more suitable   268 *fellows* equals; *men* servants   270 *kibe* chilblain   271 *put me to* make me wear   273 *candied* frozen

No better than the earth he lies upon
If he were that which now he's like – that's dead ;
Whom I with this obedient steel (three inches of it)
Can lay to bed for ever ; whiles you, doing thus,
To the perpetual wink for aye might put   279
This ancient morsel, this Sir Prudence, who
Should not upbraid our course. For all the rest,
They'll take suggestion as a cat laps milk ;
They'll tell the clock to any business that   283
We say befits the hour.

SEBASTIAN   Thy case, dear friend,
Shall be my precedent. As thou got'st Milan,
I'll come by Naples. Draw thy sword. One stroke
Shall free thee from the tribute which thou payest,
And I the King shall love thee.

ANTONIO   Draw together ;
And when I rear my hand, do you the like,
To fall it on Gonzalo.   290
        [They draw.]

SEBASTIAN   O, but one word !
        Enter Ariel, [invisible,] with music and song.

ARIEL
My master through his art foresees the danger
That you, his friend, are in, and sends me forth
(For else his project dies) to keep them living.
        Sings in Gonzalo's ear.
                While you here do snoring lie,
                Open-eyed conspiracy
                    His time doth take.
                If of life you keep a care,
                Shake off slumber and beware.
                    Awake, awake !

ANTONIO
Then let us both be sudden.

---

279 *wink* sleep   **283** *tell the clock* answer appropriately   **290** *fall it* let if fall

GONZALO [*wakes*]   Now good angels
Preserve the King!

ALONSO
Why, how now? – Ho, awake! – Why are you drawn?
Wherefore this ghastly looking?

GONZALO   What's the matter?

SEBASTIAN
304   Whiles we stood here securing your repose,
Even now, we heard a hollow burst of bellowing
Like bulls, or rather lions. Did't not wake you?
It struck mine ear most terribly.

ALONSO   I heard nothing.

ANTONIO
O, 'twas a din to fright a monster's ear,
To make an earthquake! Sure it was the roar
Of a whole herd of lions.

ALONSO   Heard you this, Gonzalo?

GONZALO
Upon mine honor, sir, I heard a humming,
And that a strange one too, which did awake me.
I shaked you, sir, and cried. As mine eyes opened,
I saw their weapons drawn. There was a noise,
That's verily. 'Tis best we stand upon our guard,
Or that we quit this place. Let's draw our weapons.

ALONSO
Lead off this ground, and let's make further search
For my poor son.

GONZALO   Heavens keep him from these beasts!
For he is sure i' th' island.

ALONSO   Lead away.

ARIEL
Prospero my lord shall know what I have done.
So, King, go safely on to seek thy son.   *Exeunt*

*

304 *securing* keeping watch over

*Enter Caliban with a burden of wood. A noise of
thunder heard.*　　　　　　　　　　　　　　　II, ii

CALIBAN

All the infections that the sun sucks up
From bogs, fens, flats, on Prosper fall, and make him
By inchmeal a disease! His spirits hear me,　　　　　3
And yet I needs must curse. But they'll nor pinch,　　4
Fright me with urchin-shows, pitch me i' th' mire,　　5
Nor lead me, like a firebrand, in the dark　　　　　　6
Out of my way, unless he bid 'em; but
For every trifle are they set upon me;
Sometime like apes that mow and chatter at me,　　　9
And after bite me; then like hedgehogs which
Lie tumbling in my barefoot way and mount
Their pricks at my footfall; sometime am I
All wound with adders, who with cloven tongues
Do hiss me into madness.
　　　　Enter Trinculo.　　　Lo, now, lo!
Here comes a spirit of his, and to torment me
For bringing wood in slowly. I'll fall flat.
Perchance he will not mind me.
　　　[*Lies down.*]

TRINCULO Here's neither bush nor shrub to bear off any　18
weather at all, and another storm brewing: I hear it sing
i' th' wind. Yond same black cloud, yond huge one,
looks like a foul bombard that would shed his liquor.　21
If it should thunder as it did before, I know not where
to hide my head. Yond same cloud cannot choose but
fall by pailfuls. What have we here? a man or a fish?
dead or alive? A fish: he smells like a fish; a very ancient
and fishlike smell; a kind of not of the newest poor-John.　26
A strange fish! Were I in England now, as once I was,

II, ii A place near Prospero's cell　3 *By inchmeal* inch by inch　4 *nor* neither
5 *urchin-shows* apparitions in the form of hedgehogs　6 *like a firebrand* in the
form of a will-o'-the-wisp　9 *mow* make faces　18 *bear off* ward off　21
bombard leather bottle; *his* its　26 *poor-John* dried hake

28   and had but this fish painted, not a holiday fool there but
        would give a piece of silver. There would this monster
30   make a man : any strange beast there makes a man. When
31   they will not give a doit to relieve a lame beggar, they
        will lay out ten to see a dead Indian. Legged like a man!
        and his fins like arms! Warm, o' my troth! I do now let
        loose my opinion, hold it no longer : this is no fish, but
        an islander, that hath lately suffered by a thunderbolt.
        [Thunder.] Alas, the storm is come again! My best way
37   is to creep under his gaberdine : there is no other shelter
        hereabout. Misery acquaints a man with strange bed-
        fellows. I will here shroud till the dregs of the storm be
        past.
            [Creeps under Caliban's garment.]
            Enter Stephano, singing [with a bottle in his hand].
STEPHANO   I shall no more to sea, to sea ;
                    Here shall I die ashore.
        This is a very scurvy tune to sing at a man's funeral.
        Well, here's my comfort.
            Drinks.

        The master, the swabber, the boatswain, and I,
            The gunner, and his mate,
        Loved Mall, Meg, and Marian, and Margery,
            But none of us cared for Kate.
            For she had a tongue with a tang,
50   Would cry to a sailor 'Go hang!'
        She loved not the savor of tar nor of pitch ;
        Yet a tailor might scratch her where'er she did itch.
            Then to sea, boys, and let her go hang!

        This is a scurvy tune too ; but here's my comfort.
            Drinks.

        28 painted i.e. on a signboard outside a booth at a fair   30 make a man (also
        with sense of 'make a man's fortune')   31 doit small coin   37 gaberdine
        cloak

66

CALIBAN Do not torment me! O!

STEPHANO What's the matter? Have we devils here? Do
you put tricks upon's with savages and men of Inde, ha?
I have not scaped drowning to be afeard now of your
four legs; for it hath been said, 'As proper a man as ever
went on four legs cannot make him give ground'; and 60
it shall be said so again, while Stephano breathes at
nostrils.

CALIBAN The spirit torments me. O!

STEPHANO This is some monster of the isle, with four
legs, who hath got, as I take it, an ague. Where the devil
should he learn our language? I will give him some
relief, if it be but for that. If I can recover him, and keep
him tame, and get to Naples with him, he's a present
for any emperor that ever trod on neat's leather.   69

CALIBAN Do not torment me, prithee; I'll bring my
wood home faster.

STEPHANO He's in his fit now and does not talk after the
wisest. He shall taste of my bottle: if he have never
drunk wine afore, it will go near to remove his fit. If I
can recover him and keep him tame, I will not take too 75
much for him; he shall pay for him that hath him, and
that soundly.

CALIBAN
Thou dost me yet but little hurt.
Thou wilt anon; I know it by thy trembling.   79
Now Prosper works upon thee.

STEPHANO Come on your ways: open your mouth: here
is that which will give language to you, cat. Open your 82
mouth. This will shake your shaking, I can tell you, and
that soundly. *[Gives Caliban drink.]* You cannot tell
who's your friend. Open your chaps again.   85

TRINCULO I should know that voice. It should be – but
he is drowned; and these are devils. O, defend me!

69 *neat's leather* cowhide   75–76 *not take too much* i.e. take all I can get
79 *anon* soon   82 *cat* (alluding to the proverb 'Liquor will make a cat talk')
85 *chaps* jaws

STEPHANO Four legs and two voices – a most delicate
monster! His forward voice now is to speak well of his
friend; his backward voice is to utter foul speeches and
to detract. If all the wine in my bottle will recover him,
I will help his ague. Come! *[Gives drink.]* Amen! I will
pour some in thy other mouth.

TRINCULO Stephano!

STEPHANO Doth thy other mouth call me? Mercy,
mercy! This is a devil, and no monster. I will leave
97   him; I have no long spoon.

TRINCULO Stephano! If thou beest Stephano, touch me
and speak to me; for I am Trinculo – be not afeard – thy
good friend Trinculo.

STEPHANO If thou beest Trinculo, come forth. I'll pull
thee by the lesser legs. If any be Trinculo's legs, these
are they. *[Draws him out from under Caliban's garment.]*
Thou art very Trinculo indeed: how cam'st thou to be
105   the siege of this mooncalf? Can he vent Trinculos?

TRINCULO I took him to be killed with a thunder-stroke.
But art thou not drowned, Stephano? I hope now thou
art not drowned. Is the storm overblown? I hid me
under the dead mooncalf's gaberdine for fear of the
storm. And art thou living, Stephano? O Stephano,
two Neapolitans scaped!

STEPHANO Prithee do not turn me about: my stomach is
not constant.

CALIBAN *[aside]*
114   These be fine things, an if they be not sprites.
That's a brave god and bears celestial liquor.
I will kneel to him.

STEPHANO How didst thou scape? How cam'st thou
hither? Swear by this bottle how thou cam'st hither. I
escaped upon a butt of sack which the sailors heaved
o'erboard, by this bottle, which I made of the bark of a

---

97 *spoon* (alluding to the proverb 'He who sups with the devil must have a
long spoon')   105 *siege* excrement; *mooncalf* monstrosity   114 *an if* if

tree with mine own hands since I was cast ashore.

CALIBAN I'll swear upon that bottle to be thy true subject, for the liquor is not earthly.

STEPHANO Here! Swear then how thou escapedst.

TRINCULO Swum ashore, man, like a duck. I can swim like a duck, I'll be sworn.

STEPHANO Here, kiss the book. *[Gives him drink.]* Though   127
thou canst swim like a duck, thou art made like a goose.   128

TRINCULO O Stephano, hast any more of this?

STEPHANO The whole butt, man: my cellar is in a rock by th' seaside, where my wine is hid. How now, mooncalf? How does thine ague?

CALIBAN Hast thou not dropped from heaven?

STEPHANO Out o' th' moon, I do assure thee. I was the Man i' th' Moon when time was.   135

CALIBAN
I have seen thee in her, and I do adore thee.
My mistress showed me thee, and thy dog, and thy bush.

STEPHANO Come, swear to that; kiss the book. I will furnish it anon with new contents. Swear.
   [Caliban drinks.]

TRINCULO By this good light, this is a very shallow monster! I afeard of him? A very weak monster! The Man i' th' Moon? A most poor credulous monster! – Well drawn, monster, in good sooth!

CALIBAN
I'll show thee every fertile inch o' th' island;
And I will kiss thy foot. I prithee be my god.

TRINCULO By this light, a most perfidious and drunken monster! When's god's asleep, he'll rob his bottle.

CALIBAN
I'll kiss thy foot. I'll swear myself thy subject.

STEPHANO Come on then. Down, and swear!

TRINCULO I shall laugh myself to death at this puppy-   150

---

127 *book* i.e. bottle   128 *like a goose* i.e. with a long neck   135 *when time was* once upon a time

headed monster. A most scurvy monster! I could find
in my heart to beat him –

STEPHANO Come, kiss.

TRINCULO But that the poor monster 's in drink. An
abominable monster!

CALIBAN

I'll show thee the best springs; I'll pluck thee berries;
I'll fish for thee, and get thee wood enough.
A plague upon the tyrant that I serve!
I'll bear him no more sticks, but follow thee,
Thou wondrous man.

TRINCULO A most ridiculous monster, to make a wonder
of a poor drunkard!

CALIBAN

163   I prithee let me bring thee where crabs grow;
164   And I with my long nails will dig thee pignuts,
Show thee a jay's nest, and instruct thee how
To snare the nimble marmoset; I'll bring thee
To clust'ring filberts, and sometimes I'll get thee
168   Young scamels from the rock. Wilt thou go with me?

STEPHANO I prithee now, lead the way without any more
talking. Trinculo, the King and all our company else
171   being drowned, we will inherit here. Here, bear my
172   bottle. Fellow Trinculo, we'll fill him by and by again.
        Caliban sings drunkenly.

CALIBAN Farewell, master; farewell, farewell!

TRINCULO A howling monster! a drunken monster!

CALIBAN

No more dams I'll make for fish,
        Nor fetch in firing
        At requiring,
178   Nor scrape trenchering, nor wash dish.

---

163 *crabs* crab apples   164 *pignuts* peanuts   168 *scamels* (unexplained, but
clearly either a shellfish or a rock-nesting bird; perhaps a misprint for 'sea-
mels,' sea mews)   171 *inherit* take possession   172 *by and by* soon   178
trenchering trenchers, wooden plates

'Ban, 'Ban, Ca – Caliban
  Has a new master : get a new man.
Freedom, high-day ! high-day, freedom ! freedom, high-
day, freedom !
STEPHANO O brave monster ! lead the way.   *Exeunt.*

*

   Enter Ferdinand, bearing a log.   III, i
FERDINAND
  There be some sports are painful, and their labor   1
  Delight in them sets off ; some kinds of baseness   2
  Are nobly undergone, and most poor matters   3
  Point to rich ends. This my mean task
  Would be as heavy to me as odious, but
  The mistress which I serve quickens what's dead   6
  And makes my labors pleasures. O, she is
  Ten times more gentle than her father's crabbèd ;
  And he's composed of harshness ! I must remove
  Some thousands of these logs and pile them up,
  Upon a sore injunction. My sweet mistress   11
  Weeps when she sees me work, and says such baseness
  Had never like executor. I forget ;
  But these sweet thoughts do even refresh my labors
  Most busy least, when I do it.   15
   Enter Miranda ; and Prospero [behind, unseen].
MIRANDA   Alas, now pray you
  Work not so hard ! I would the lightning had
  Burnt up those logs that you are enjoined to pile !
  Pray set it down and rest you. When this burns,
  'Twill weep for having wearied you. My father   19
  Is hard at study : pray now rest yourself.
  He's safe for these three hours.

III, i Before Prospero's cell   1 *painful* strenuous   2 *sets off* makes greater
by contrast   3 *matters* affairs   6 *quickens* brings to life   11 *sore injunction*
grievous command   15 *least* i.e. least conscious of being busy (F reads
'lest')   19 *weep* i.e. exude resin

FERDINAND   O most dear mistress,
The sun will set before I shall discharge
What I must strive to do.

MIRANDA   If you'll sit down,
I'll bear your logs the while. Pray give me that:
I'll carry it to the pile.

FERDINAND   No, precious creature:
I had rather crack my sinews, break my back,
Than you should such dishonor undergo
While I sit lazy by.

MIRANDA   It would become me
As well as it does you; and I should do it
With much more ease; for my good will is to it,
And yours it is against.

PROSPERO [aside]   Poor worm, thou art infected!
32   This visitation shows it.

MIRANDA   You look wearily.

FERDINAND
No, noble mistress: 'tis fresh morning with me
When you are by at night. I do beseech you,
Chiefly that I might set it in my prayers,
What is your name?

MIRANDA   Miranda. O my father,
37   I have broke your hest to say so!

FERDINAND   Admired Miranda!
38   Indeed the top of admiration, worth
What's dearest to the world! Full many a lady
40   I have eyed with best regard, and many a time
Th' harmony of their tongues hath into bondage
42   Brought my too diligent ear; for several virtues
Have I liked several women; never any
44   With so full soul but some defect in her
45   Did quarrel with the noblest grace she owed,

---

32 *visitation* (1) visit, (2) attack of plague (in the metaphor of *infected*)   37
hest command   38 *admiration* wonder, astonishment (the name Miranda
means wonderful woman; cf. I, ii, 427)   40 *best regard* highest approval   42
several different   44 *With ... soul* i.e. so wholeheartedly   45 *owed* owned

And put it to the foil. But you, O you,   46
So perfect and so peerless, are created
Of every creature's best.

MIRANDA   I do not know
One of my sex; no woman's face remember,
Save, from my glass, mine own; nor have I seen
More that I may call men than you, good friend,
And my dear father. How features are abroad   52
I am skilless of; but, by my modesty   53
(The jewel in my dower), I would not wish
Any companion in the world but you;
Nor can imagination form a shape,
Besides yourself, to like of. But I prattle   57
Something too wildly, and my father's precepts
I therein do forget.

FERDINAND   I am, in my condition,   59
A prince, Miranda; I do think, a king
(I would not so), and would no more endure
This wooden slavery than to suffer
The fleshfly blow my mouth. Hear my soul speak!
The very instant that I saw you, did
My heart fly to your service; there resides,
To make me slave to it; and for your sake
Am I this patient log-man.

MIRANDA   Do you love me?

FERDINAND
O heaven, O earth, bear witness to this sound,
And crown what I profess with kind event   69
If I speak true! if hollowly, invert
What best is boded me to mischief! I,
Beyond all limit of what else i' th' world,
Do love, prize, honor you.

MIRANDA   I am a fool
To weep at what I am glad of.

46 *foil* (1) overthrow, (2) contrast   52 *abroad* elsewhere   53 *skilless* ignorant
57 *like of* compare to   59 *condition* situation in the world   69 *kind event*
favorable outcome

PROSPERO *[aside]*   Fair encounter
 Of two most rare affections! Heavens rain grace
 On that which breeds between 'em!
FERDINAND   Wherefore weep you?
MIRANDA
 At mine unworthiness, that dare not offer
 What I desire to give, and much less take
79 What I shall die to want. But this is trifling;
 And all the more it seeks to hide itself,
81 The bigger bulk it shows. Hence, bashful cunning,
 And prompt me, plain and holy innocence!
 I am your wife, if you will marry me;
84 If not, I'll die your maid. To be your fellow
 You may deny me; but I'll be your servant,
 Whether you will or no.
FERDINAND   My mistress, dearest,
 And I thus humble ever.
MIRANDA   My husband then?
FERDINAND
 Ay, with a heart as willing
89 As bondage e'er of freedom. Here's my hand.
MIRANDA
 And mine, with my heart in't; and now farewell
 Till half an hour hence.
FERDINAND   A thousand thousand!
     Exeunt [Ferdinand and Miranda severally].
PROSPERO
 So glad of this as they I cannot be,
93 Who are surprised withal; but my rejoicing
 At nothing can be more. I'll to my book;
 For yet ere supper time must I perform
96 Much business appertaining.   *Exit.*

*

79 *want* lack   **81** *bashful cunning* i.e. coyness   **84** *fellow* equal   **89** *of free-dom* i.e. to win freedom   **93** *surprised withal* taken unaware by it   **96** *appertaining* relevant

Enter Caliban, Stephano, and Trinculo.   III, ii

STEPHANO Tell not me! When the butt is out, we will
   drink water; not a drop before. Therefore bear up and   2
   board 'em! Servant monster, drink to me.

TRINCULO Servant monster? The folly of this island!
   They say there's but five upon this isle: we are three of
   them. If th' other two be brained like us, the state
   totters.

STEPHANO Drink, servant monster, when I bid thee:
   thy eyes are almost set in thy head.

TRINCULO Where should they be set else? He were a
   brave monster indeed if they were set in his tail.

STEPHANO My man-monster hath drowned his tongue
   in sack. For my part, the sea cannot drown me. I swam,
   ere I could recover the shore, five-and-thirty leagues off   13
   and on, by this light. Thou shalt be my lieutenant,
   monster, or my standard.   15

TRINCULO Your lieutenant, if you list; he's no standard.   16

STEPHANO We'll not run, Monsieur Monster.   17

TRINCULO Nor go neither; but you'll lie like dogs, and   18
   yet say nothing neither.

STEPHANO Mooncalf, speak once in thy life, if thou beest
   a good mooncalf.

CALIBAN
   How does thy honor? Let me lick thy shoe.
   I'll not serve him; he is not valiant.

TRINCULO Thou liest, most ignorant monster: I am in
   case to justle a constable. Why, thou deboshed fish thou,   25
   was there ever man a coward that hath drunk so much
   sack as I to-day? Wilt thou tell a monstrous lie, being
   but half a fish and half a monster?

III, ii Another part of the island   **2–3** *bear . . . 'em* i.e. drink up (Caliban
has almost 'passed out')   **13** *recover* reach   **15** *standard* ensign   **16** *no
standard* i.e. incapable of standing up   **17, 18** *run, lie* (secondary meanings
of) make water and excrete   **18** *go* walk   **25** *case* fit condition; *deboshed*
debauched

CALIBAN Lo, how he mocks me! Wilt thou let him, my
    lord?

TRINCULO 'Lord' quoth he? That a monster should be
32 such a natural!

CALIBAN
    Lo, lo, again! Bite him to death, I prithee.

STEPHANO Trinculo, keep a good tongue in your head. If
    you prove a mutineer – the next tree! The poor mon-
    ster's my subject, and he shall not suffer indignity.

CALIBAN
    I thank my noble lord. Wilt thou be pleased
    To hearken once again to the suit I made to thee?

STEPHANO Marry, will I. Kneel and repeat it; I will
40 stand, and so shall Trinculo.
            Enter Ariel, invisible.

CALIBAN
    As I told thee before, I am subject to a tyrant,
    A sorcerer, that by his cunning hath
    Cheated me of the island.

ARIEL   Thou liest.

CALIBAN
    Thou liest, thou jesting monkey thou!
    I would my valiant master would destroy thee.
    I do not lie.

STEPHANO Trinculo, if you trouble him any more in's
    tale, by this hand, I will supplant some of your teeth.

TRINCULO Why, I said nothing.

STEPHANO Mum then, and no more. – Proceed.

CALIBAN
    I say by sorcery he got this isle;
    From me he got it. If thy greatness will
    Revenge it on him – for I know thou dar'st,
54 But this thing dare not –

STEPHANO That's most certain.

---

32 *natural* fool 40 s.d. *invisible* ('a robe for to go invisible' is listed in an
Elizabethan stage account) 54 *this thing* i.e. himself (or perhaps Trinculo)

CALIBAN
Thou shalt be lord of it, and I'll serve thee.

STEPHANO
How now shall this be compassed?
Canst thou bring me to the party?   58

CALIBAN
Yea, yea, my lord! I'll yield him thee asleep,
Where thou mayst knock a nail into his head.

ARIEL Thou liest; thou canst not.

CALIBAN
What a pied ninny's this! Thou scurvy patch!   62
I do beseech thy greatness give him blows
And take his bottle from him. When that's gone,
He shall drink naught but brine, for I'll not show him
Where the quick freshes are.   66

STEPHANO Trinculo, run into no further danger: inter-
rupt the monster one word further and, by this hand, I'll
turn my mercy out o' doors and make a stockfish of thee   69

TRINCULO Why, what did I? I did nothing. I'll go
farther off.

STEPHANO Didst thou not say he lied?

ARIEL Thou liest.

STEPHANO Do I so? Take thou that! [*Strikes Trinculo.*]
As you like this, give me the lie another time.

TRINCULO I did not give the lie. Out o' your wits, and
hearing too? A pox o' your bottle! This can sack and
drinking do. A murrain on your monster, and the devil   77
take your fingers!

CALIBAN Ha, ha, ha!

STEPHANO Now forward with your tale. – Prithee stand
further off.

CALIBAN
Beat him enough. After a little time
I'll beat him too.

58 *party* person   **62** *pied ninny* motley fool (Trinculo wears a jester's
costume); *patch* clown   **66** *quick freshes* fresh-water springs   **69** *stockfish*
dried cod, prepared by beating   **77** *murrain* cattle disease

Claims his humanity

STEPHANO   Stand farther. – Come, proceed.

CALIBAN

Why, as I told thee, 'tis a custom with him
I' th' afternoon to sleep ; there thou mayst brain him,
Having first seized his books, or with a log

87   Batter his skull, or paunch him with a stake,

88   Or cut his wesand with thy knife. Remember
First to possess his books ; for without them

90   He's but a sot, as I am, nor hath not
One spirit to command. They all do hate him
As rootedly as I. Burn but his books.

No diff. than Prospero w/out books.

93   He has brave utensils (for so he calls them)
Which, when he has a house, he'll deck withal.
And that most deeply to consider is
The beauty of his daughter. He himself
Calls her a nonpareil. I never saw a woman
But only Sycorax my dam and she ;
But she as far surpasseth Sycorax
As great'st does least.

100 STEPHANO   Is it so brave a lass ?

CALIBAN

Ay, lord. She will become thy bed, I warrant,
And bring thee forth brave brood.

STEPHANO Monster, I will kill this man : his daughter
and I will be king and queen, save our Graces! and
Trinculo and thyself shall be viceroys. Dost thou like
the plot, Trinculo ?

TRINCULO Excellent.

STEPHANO Give me thy hand. I am sorry I beat thee ; but
while thou liv'st, keep a good tongue in thy head.

CALIBAN

Within this half hour will he be asleep.
Wilt thou destroy him then ?

STEPHANO Ay, on mine honor.

---

87 *paunch* stab in the belly   **88** *wesand* windpipe   **90** *sot* fool   **93** *utensils*
furnishings

ARIEL
   This will I tell my master.
CALIBAN
   Thou mak'st me merry; I am full of pleasure.
   Let us be jocund. Will you troll the catch   114
   You taught me but whilere?   115
STEPHANO At thy request, monster, I will do reason, any
   reason. Come on, Trinculo, let us sing.
        Sings.
                  Flout 'em and scout 'em
                  And scout 'em and flout 'em!
                  Thought is free.

CALIBAN
   That's not the tune.   121
        Ariel plays the tune on a tabor and pipe.
STEPHANO What is this same?
TRINCULO This is the tune of our catch, played by the
   picture of Nobody.   124
STEPHANO If thou beest a man, show thyself in thy like-
   ness. If thou beest a devil, take't as thou list.   126
TRINCULO O, forgive me my sins!
STEPHANO He that dies pays all debts. I defy thee.
   Mercy upon us!
CALIBAN
   Art thou afeard?
STEPHANO No, monster, not I.
CALIBAN
   Be not afeard: the isle is full of noises,
   Sounds and sweet airs that give delight and hurt not.
   Sometimes a thousand twangling instruments
   Will hum about mine ears; and sometime voices
   That, if I then had waked after long sleep,
   Will make me sleep again; and then, in dreaming,

114 *troll the catch* sing the part-song   115 *whilere* just now   121 s.d. *tabor*
small drum worn at the side   124 *Nobody* (referring to pictures of figures
with arms and legs but no trunk, used on signs and elsewhere)   126 *take't as
thou list* i.e. suit yourself

The clouds methought would open and show riches
Ready to drop upon me, that, when I waked,
I cried to dream again.

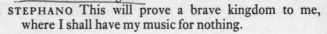

STEPHANO This will prove a brave kingdom to me,
where I shall have my music for nothing.

CALIBAN
When Prospero is destroyed.

144 STEPHANO That shall be by and by : I remember the
story.

TRINCULO The sound is going away : let's follow it, and
after do our work.

STEPHANO Lead, monster ; we'll follow. I would I could
see this taborer : he lays it on. Wilt come ?

TRINCULO I'll follow, Stephano.   *Exeunt.*

*

III, iii   *Enter Alonso, Sebastian, Antonio, Gonzalo,*
       Adrian, Francisco, &c.

GONZALO
1   By'r Lakin, I can go no further, sir :
   My old bones ache : here's a maze trod indeed
3   Through forthrights and meanders. By your patience,
   I needs must rest me.

ALONSO   Old lord, I cannot blame thee,
5   Who am myself attached with weariness
   To th' dulling of my spirits. Sit down and rest.
   Even here I will put off my hope, and keep it
   No longer for my flatterer : he is drowned
   Whom thus we stray to find ; and the sea mocks
   Our frustrate search on land. Well, let him go.

ANTONIO *[aside to Sebastian]*
   I am right glad that he's so out of hope.
   Do not for one repulse forgo the purpose

144 *by and by* right away
III, iii Another part of the island   **1** *By'r Lakin* by our Ladykin (Virgin
Mary)   **3** *forthrights* straight paths   **5** *attached* seized

That you resolved t' effect.

SEBASTIAN *[aside to Antonio]* The next advantage
Will we take throughly.   14

ANTONIO *[aside to Sebastian]* Let it be to-night;
For, now they are oppressed with travel, they
Will not nor cannot use such vigilance
As when they are fresh.

SEBASTIAN *[aside to Antonio]* I say to-night. No more.   17

> *Solemn and strange music ; and Prospero on the top
> (invisible). Enter several strange Shapes, bringing in
> a banquet ; and dance about it with gentle actions of
> salutations ; and, inviting the King &c. to eat, they
> depart.*

ALONSO
What harmony is this ? My good friends, hark !

GONZALO
Marvellous sweet music !

ALONSO
Give us kind keepers, heavens ! What were these ?   20

SEBASTIAN
A living drollery. Now I will believe   21
That there are unicorns ; that in Arabia
There is one tree, the phoenix' throne ; one phoenix
At this hour reigning there.

ANTONIO   I'll believe both ;
And what does else want credit, come to me,   25
And I'll be sworn 'tis true. Travellers ne'er did lie,
Though fools at home condemn 'em.

GONZALO   If in Naples
I should report this now, would they believe me
If I should say I saw such islanders ?
(For certes these are people of the island)
Who, though they are of monstrous shape, yet note,

---

14 *throughly* thoroughly   17 s.d. *on the top* (this may refer to an upper level
of the tiring-house of the theatre)   20 *kind keepers* guardian angels   21
living drollery puppet show with live figures   25 *want credit* lack credibility

> Their manners are more gentle, kind, than of
> Our human generation you shall find
> Many – nay, almost any.

PROSPERO *[aside]*   Honest lord,
> Thou hast said well ; for some of you there present
> Are worse than devils.

36 ALONSO   I cannot too much muse
> Such shapes, such gesture, and such sound, expressing
> (Although they want the use of tongue) a kind
> Of excellent dumb discourse.

39 PROSPERO *[aside]*   Praise in departing.

FRANCISCO
> They vanished strangely.

SEBASTIAN   No matter, since
> They have left their viands behind ; for we have
>   stomachs.
> Will't please you taste of what is here ?

ALONSO   Not I.

GONZALO
> Faith, sir, you need not fear. When we were boys,
> Who would believe that there were mountaineers
45 Dewlapped like bulls, whose throats had hanging at 'em
> Wallets of flesh ? or that there were such men
47 Whose heads stood in their breasts ? which now we find
48 Each putter-out of five for one will bring us
> Good warrant of.

ALONSO   I will stand to, and feed ;
> Although my last, no matter, since I feel
> The best is past. Brother, my lord the Duke,
> Stand to, and do as we.

---

36 *muse* wonder at   39 *Praise in departing* save your praise for the end   45
Dewlapped with skin hanging from the neck (like the goitrous Swiss
mountaineers)   47 *in their breasts* (an ancient travellers' tale; cf. *Othello* I,
iii, 144–45)   48 *putter-out . . . one* traveller depositing a sum for insurance in
London, to be repaid fivefold if he returned safely and proved he had gone to
his destination

Thunder and lightning. Enter Ariel, like a harpy ;   52
claps his wings upon the table ; and with a quaint
device the banquet vanishes.

ARIEL

You are three men of sin, whom destiny –
That hath to instrument this lower world   54
And what is in't – the never-surfeited sea
Hath caused to belch up you, and on this island,
Where man doth not inhabit, you 'mongst men
Being most unfit to live, I have made you mad ;
And even with such-like valor men hang and drown
Their proper selves.
      [Alonso, Sebastian, &c. draw their swords.]
               You fools : I and my fellows
Are ministers of Fate. The elements,
Of whom your swords are tempered, may as well
Wound the loud winds, or with bemocked-at stabs
Kill the still-closing waters, as diminish   64
One dowle that's in my plume. My fellow ministers   65
Are like invulnerable. If you could hurt,   66
Your swords are now too massy for your strengths   67
And will not be uplifted. But remember
(For that's my business to you) that you three
From Milan did supplant good Prospero ;
Exposed unto the sea, which hath requit it,   71
Him and his innocent child ; for which foul deed
The pow'rs, delaying, not forgetting, have
Incensed the seas and shores, yea, all the creatures,
Against your peace. Thee of thy son, Alonso,
They have bereft ; and do pronounce by me
Ling'ring perdition (worse than any death   77
Can be at once) shall step by step attend
You and your ways ; whose wraths to guard you from,

---

52 s.d. *quaint* ingenious   54 *to* i.e. as its   64 *still* constantly   65 *dowle* fibre
of feather-down   66 *like* also   67 *massy* massive   71 *requit* avenged; *it* i.e.
the usurpation   77 *perdition* ruin

Which here, in this most desolate isle, else falls
81 Upon your heads, is nothing but heart's sorrow
82 And a clear life ensuing.

> *He vanishes in thunder ; then, to soft music, enter the*
> *Shapes again, and dance with mocks and mows, and*
> *carrying out the table.*

PROSPERO
Bravely the figure of this harpy hast thou
84 Performed, my Ariel ; a grace it had, devouring.
85 Of my instruction hast thou nothing bated
86 In what thou hadst to say. So, with good life
87 And observation strange, my meaner ministers
88 Their several kinds have done. My high charms work,
And these, mine enemies, are all knit up
In their distractions : they now are in my pow'r ;
And in these fits I leave them, while I visit
Young Ferdinand, whom they suppose is drowned,
And his and mine loved darling.   *[Exit above.]*

GONZALO
94 I' th' name of something holy, sir, why stand you
In this strange stare ?

95 ALONSO   O, it is monstrous, monstrous !
Methought the billows spoke and told me of it ;
The winds did sing it to me ; and the thunder,
That deep and dreadful organ pipe, pronounced
99 The name of Prosper ; it did bass my trespass.
Therefore my son i' th' ooze is bedded ; and
I'll seek him deeper than e'er plummet sounded
And with him there lie mudded.   *Exit.*

SEBASTIAN   But one fiend at a time,
I'll fight their legions o'er !

---

81 *heart's sorrow* repentance **82** *clear* innocent; **s.d.** *mocks and mows*
grimaces and gestures **84** *devouring* i.e. making the banquet disappear **85**
bated omitted **86** *good life* realistic acting **87** *observation strange* wonder-
fully close attention **88** *several kinds* separate parts **94** *why* (Gonzalo has
not heard Ariel's speech) **95** *it* i.e. my sin **99** *bass* proclaim in deep tones
(literally, provide the bass part for)

ANTONIO   I'll be thy second.
                        Exeunt [Sebastian and Antonio].

GONZALO
    All three of them are desperate : their great guilt,
    Like poison given to work a great time after,
    Now gins to bite the spirits. I do beseech you,
    That are of suppler joints, follow them swiftly
    And hinder them from what this ecstasy   108
    May now provoke them to.
ADRIAN   Follow, I pray you.
                        Exeunt omnes.

                        *

    Enter Prospero, Ferdinand, and Miranda.   IV, i

PROSPERO
    If I have too austerely punished you,
    Your compensation makes amends ; for I
    Have given you here a third of mine own life,   3
    Or that for which I live ; who once again
    I tender to thy hand. All thy vexations
    Were but my trials of thy love, and thou
    Hast strangely stood the test. Here, afore heaven,   7
    I ratify this my rich gift. O Ferdinand,
    Do not smile at me that I boast her off,   9
    For thou shalt find she will outstrip all praise
    And make it halt behind her.   11
FERDINAND   I do believe it
    Against an oracle.   12
PROSPERO
    Then, as my gift, and thine own acquisition
    Worthily purchased, take my daughter. But
    If thou dost break her virgin-knot before

---

108 *ecstasy* madness
IV, i Before Prospero's cell   3 *third* (Prospero's love, his knowledge and
his power being the other two-thirds?)   7 *strangely* in a rare fashion
9 *boast her off* boast about her   11 *halt* limp   12 *Against an oracle* even
if an oracle denied it

16   All sanctimonious ceremonies may
      With full and holy rite be minist'red,
18   No sweet aspersion shall the heavens let fall
19   To make this contract grow; but barren hate,
      Sour-eyed disdain, and discord shall bestrew
      The union of your bed with weeds so loathly
      That you shall hate it both. Therefore take heed,
      As Hymen's lamp shall light you.

FERDINAND   As I hope
      For quiet days, fair issue, and long life,
      With such love as 'tis now, the murkiest den,
26   The most opportune place, the strong'st suggestion
27   Our worser genius can, shall never melt
      Mine honor into lust, to take away
      The edge of that day's celebration
30   When I shall think or Phoebus' steeds are foundered
      Or Night kept chained below.

PROSPERO   Fairly spoke.
      Sit then and talk with her; she is thine own.
      What, Ariel! My industrious servant, Ariel!
        Enter Ariel.

ARIEL
      What would my potent master? Here I am.

PROSPERO
      Thou and thy meaner fellows your last service
      Did worthily perform; and I must use you
37   In such another trick. Go bring the rabble,
      O'er whom I give thee pow'r, here to this place.
      Incite them to quick motion; for I must
      Bestow upon the eyes of this young couple
41   Some vanity of mine art; it is my promise,
      And they expect it from me.

ARIEL   Presently?

---

16 *sanctimonious* holy   18 *aspersion* blessing, like rain on crops   19 *grow* become fruitful   26 *opportune* (accent second syllable)   27 *worser genius can* bad angel can make   30 *or . . . foundered* either the sun-god's horses are lame   37 *rabble* rank and file   41 *vanity* show

PROSPERO
  Ay, with a twink.

ARIEL
  Before you can say 'Come' and 'Go,'
  And breathe twice and cry, 'So, so,'
  Each one, tripping on his toe,
  Will be here with mop and mow.   47
  Do you love me, master ? No ?

PROSPERO
  Dearly, my delicate Ariel. Do not approach
  Till thou dost hear me call.

ARIEL   Well : I conceive.   *Exit.* 50

PROSPERO
  Look thou be true : do not give dalliance   51
  Too much the rein : the strongest oaths are straw
  To th' fire i' th' blood. Be more abstemious,
  Or else good night your vow !

FERDINAND   I warrant you, sir.
  The white cold virgin snow upon my heart
  Abates the ardor of my liver.   56

PROSPERO   Well.
  Now come, my Ariel : bring a corollary   57
  Rather than want a spirit. Appear, and pertly !   58
  No tongue ! All eyes ! Be silent.
        Soft music. Enter Iris.

IRIS
  Ceres, most bounteous lady, thy rich leas   60
  Of wheat, rye, barley, fetches, oats, and pease ;   61
  Thy turfy mountains, where live nibbling sheep,
  And flat meads thatched with stover, them to keep ; 63
  Thy banks with pionèd and twillèd brims,   64

47 *mop and mow* antics and gestures   50 *conceive* understand   51 *be true*
(Prospero appears to have caught the lovers in an embrace)   56 *liver* (sup-
posed seat of sexual passion)   57 *corollary* surplus   58 *want* lack; *pertly*
briskly   60 *Iris* goddess of the rainbow and female messenger of the gods
61 *fetches* vetch   63 *stover* winter food for stock   64 *pionèd and twillèd* dug
under by the current and protected by woven layers of branches (sometimes
emended to 'peonied and lilied')

Which spongy April at thy hest betrims
66 To make cold nymphs chaste crowns ; and thy broom groves,
    Whose shadow the dismissèd bachelor loves,
68 Being lasslorn ; thy pole-clipt vineyard ;
69 And thy sea-marge, sterile and rocky-hard,
70 Where thou thyself dost air – the queen o' th' sky,
    Whose wat'ry arch and messenger am I,
    Bids thee leave these, and with her sovereign grace,
73 Here on this grass-plot, in this very place,
74 To come and sport : her peacocks fly amain.
    Approach, rich Ceres, her to entertain.
        Enter Ceres.

CERES
    Hail, many-colorèd messenger, that ne'er
    Dost disobey the wife of Jupiter,
    Who, with thy saffron wings, upon my flow'rs
    Diffusest honey drops, refreshing show'rs,
    And with each end of thy blue bow dost crown
81 My bosky acres and my unshrubbed down,
    Rich scarf to my proud earth – why hath thy queen
    Summoned me hither to this short-grassed green ?

IRIS
    A contract of true love to celebrate
85 And some donation freely to estate
    On the blessed lovers.

CERES   Tell me, heavenly bow,
87 If Venus or her son, as thou dost know,
    Do now attend the queen ? Since they did plot
89 The means that dusky Dis my daughter got,
90 Her and her blind boy's scandalled company

66 *broom groves* clumps of gorse   68 *pole-clipt* pruned ; *vineyard* (probably a trisyllable)   69 *sea-marge* shore   70 *queen* i.e. Juno   73 *Here . . . place* (in F a stage direction at this point reads 'Juno descends')   74 *peacocks* (these were sacred to Juno, as doves were to Venus [l. 94], and drew her chariot)   81 *bosky* wooded   85 *estate* bestow   87 *her son* Cupid, often represented as blind or blindfolded   89 *means* i.e. the abduction of Proserpine, Ceres' daughter, by Pluto (Dis), god of the lower (*dusky*) world   90 *scandalled* disgraceful

I have forsworn.

IRIS   Of her society
    Be not afraid : I met her Deity   92
    Cutting the clouds towards Paphos, and her son   93
    Dove-drawn with her. Here thought they to have done
    Some wanton charm upon this man and maid,
    Whose vows are, that no bed-right shall be paid
    Till Hymen's torch be lighted ; but in vain.
    Mars's hot minion is returned again ;   98
    Her waspish-headed son has broke his arrows,   99
    Swears he will shoot no more, but play with sparrows
    And be a boy right out.   101
            [Enter Juno.]

CERES   Highest queen of state,
    Great Juno, comes ; I know her by her gait.

JUNO
    How does my bounteous sister ? Go with me
    To bless this twain, that they may prosperous be
    And honored in their issue.
            They sing.

JUNO   Honor, riches, marriage blessing,
            Long continuance, and increasing,
            Hourly joys be still upon you !   108
            Juno sings her blessings on you.

[CERES]   Earth's increase, foison plenty,   110
            Barns and garners never empty,
            Vines with clust'ring bunches growing,
            Plants with goodly burden bowing ;
            Spring come to you at the farthest
            In the very end of harvest.
            Scarcity and want shall shun you,
            Ceres' blessing so is on you.

---

92 *her Deity* i.e. her Divine Majesty   93 *Paphos* (in Cyprus, center of Venus'
cult)   98 *Mars's . . . again* the lustful mistress of Mars (Venus) has gone
back to where she came from   99 *waspish-headed* spiteful and inclined to
sting (with his arrows)   101 *right out* outright   108 *still* constantly   110
foison abundance

89

FERDINAND
 This is a most majestic vision, and
 Harmonious charmingly. May I be bold
 To think these spirits ?
PROSPERO   Spirits, which by mine art
 I have from their confines called to enact
 My present fancies.
FERDINAND   Let me live here ever !
123 So rare a wond'red father and a wise
 Makes this place Paradise.
   Juno and Ceres whisper, and send Iris on employment.
PROSPERO   Sweet now, silence !
 Juno and Ceres whisper seriously.
 There's something else to do. Hush and be mute,
 Or else our spell is marred.
IRIS
128 You nymphs, called Naiades, of the windring brooks,
 With your sedged crowns and ever-harmless looks,
130 Leave your crisp channels, and on this green land
 Answer your summons ; Juno does command.
 Come, temperate nymphs, and help to celebrate
 A contract of true love : be not too late.
   Enter certain Nymphs.
 You sunburned sicklemen, of August weary,
 Come hither from the furrow and be merry.
 Make holiday : your rye-straw hats put on,
 And these fresh nymphs encounter every one
138 In country footing.
   Enter certain Reapers, properly habited. They join
   with the Nymphs in a graceful dance ; towards the end
   whereof Prospero starts suddenly and speaks ; after
   which, to a strange, hollow, and confused noise, they
   heavily vanish.

123 *wond'red* wonderful 128 *windring* winding and wandering 130 *crisp*
rippling 138 s.d. *speaks* (thereby dissolving the scene, which depended on
silence)

PROSPERO *[aside]*
      I had forgot that foul conspiracy
      Of the beast Caliban and his confederates
      Against my life : the minute of their plot
      Is almost come.
              [To the Spirits] Well done! Avoid! No more!   142

FERDINAND
      This is strange. Your father's in some passion
      That works him strongly.

MIRANDA   Never till this day
      Saw I him touched with anger so distempered.

PROSPERO
      You do look, my son, in a moved sort,   146
      As if you were dismayed : be cheerful, sir.
      Our revels now are ended. These our actors,   148
      As I foretold you, were all spirits and
      Are melted into air, into thin air ;
      And, like the baseless fabric of this vision,   151
      The cloud-capped tow'rs, the gorgeous palaces,
      The solemn temples, the great globe itself,
      Yea, all which it inherit, shall dissolve,   154
      And, like this insubstantial pageant faded,
      Leave not a rack behind. We are such stuff   156
      As dreams are made on, and our little life   157
      Is rounded with a sleep. Sir, I am vexed.
      Bear with my weakness : my old brain is troubled.
      Be not disturbed with my infirmity.
      If you be pleased, retire into my cell
      And there repose. A turn or two I'll walk
      To still my beating mind.

FERDINAND, MIRANDA   We wish your peace.
                              Exit [Ferdinand with Miranda].
        Enter Ariel.

142 *Avoid* be off   146 *moved sort* troubled state   148 *revels* pageants   151
baseless insubstantial, non-material   154 *it inherit* occupy it   156 *rack*
wisp of cloud   157 *on* of

PROSPERO
Come with a thought! I thank thee, Ariel. Come.
ARIEL
Thy thoughts I cleave to. What's thy pleasure?
PROSPERO   Spirit,
We must prepare to meet with Caliban.
ARIEL
167 Ay, my commander: when I presented Ceres,
I thought to have told thee of it, but I feared
Lest I might anger thee.
PROSPERO
170 Say again, where didst thou leave these varlets?
ARIEL
I told you, sir, they were redhot with drinking;
So full of valor that they smote the air
For breathing in their faces, beat the ground
For kissing of their feet; yet always bending
Towards their project. Then I beat my tabor;
176 At which like unbacked colts they pricked their ears,
177 Advanced their eyelids, lifted up their noses
As they smelt music. So I charmed their ears
That calf-like they my lowing followed through
180 Toothed briers, sharp furzes, pricking goss, and thorns,
Which ent'red their frail shins. At last I left them
182 I' th' filthy mantled pool beyond your cell,
There dancing up to th' chins, that the foul lake
O'erstunk their feet.
PROSPERO   This was well done, my bird.
Thy shape invisible retain thou still.
The trumpery in my house, go bring it hither
187 For stale to catch these thieves.
ARIEL   I go, I go.   *Exit*.
PROSPERO
A devil, a born devil, on whose nature

167 *presented* acted the part of (?), introduced (?)   170 *varlets* ruffians   176
unbacked unbroken   177 *Advanced* lifted up   180 *goss* gorse   182 *mantled*
scummed   187 *stale* decoy

Nurture can never stick : on whom my pains,
Humanely taken, all, all lost, quite lost!
And as with age his body uglier grows,
So his mind cankers. I will plague them all,   192
Even to roaring.

> *Enter Ariel, loaden with glistering apparel, &c.*

                    Come, hang them on this line.   193

> *[Prospero and Ariel remain, invisible.] Enter Caliban,*
> *Stephano, and Trinculo, all wet.*

CALIBAN
Pray you tread softly, that the blind mole may not
Hear a foot fall. We now are near his cell.

STEPHANO Monster, your fairy, which you say is a harmless fairy, has done little better than played the Jack 197
with us.

TRINCULO Monster, I do smell all horse-piss, at which
my nose is in great indignation.

STEPHANO So is mine. Do you hear, monster? If I
should take a displeasure against you, look you –

TRINCULO Thou wert but a lost monster.

CALIBAN
Good my lord, give me thy favor still.
Be patient, for the prize I'll bring thee to
Shall hoodwink this mischance. Therefore speak softly.   205
All's hushed as midnight yet.

TRINCULO Ay, but to lose our bottles in the pool –

STEPHANO There is not only disgrace and dishonor in
that, monster, but an infinite loss.

TRINCULO That's more to me than my wetting. Yet this
is your harmless fairy, monster.

STEPHANO I will fetch off my bottle, though I be o'er
ears for my labor.

CALIBAN
Prithee, my king, be quiet. Seest thou here?

---

192 *cankers* festers   193 *line* lime or linden-tree, or perhaps a clothesline
made of hair   197 *Jack* (1) knave, (2) jack-o'-lantern, will-o'-the-wisp   **205**
hoodwink cover over

This is the mouth o' th' cell. No noise, and enter.
Do that good mischief which may make this island
Thine own for ever, and I, thy Caliban,
For aye thy foot-licker.

STEPHANO Give me thy hand. I do begin to have bloody
thoughts.

221 TRINCULO O King Stephano! O peer! O worthy Stephano, look what a wardrobe here is for thee!

CALIBAN
Let it alone, thou fool! It is but trash.

TRINCULO O, ho, monster! we know what belongs to a
225   frippery. O King Stephano!

STEPHANO Put off that gown, Trinculo: by this hand,
I'll have that gown!

TRINCULO Thy Grace shall have it.

CALIBAN
The dropsy drown this fool! What do you mean
230   To dote thus on such luggage? Let't alone,
And do the murder first. If he awake,
From toe to crown he'll fill our skins with pinches,
Make us strange stuff.

234 STEPHANO Be you quiet, monster. Mistress line, is not
this my jerkin? *[Takes it down.]* Now is the jerkin under
the line. Now, jerkin, you are like to lose your hair and
prove a bald jerkin.

238 TRINCULO Do, do! We steal by line and level, an't like
your Grace.

STEPHANO I thank thee for that jest. Here's a garment
for't. Wit shall not go unrewarded while I am king of
242   this country. 'Steal by line and level' is an excellent pass
of pate. There's another garment for't.

221 *peer* (referring to the song 'King Stephen was a worthy peer,' quoted in
Othello II, iii, 84–91)   225 *frippery* old-clothes shop   230 *luggage* junk
234 ff. (the jokes are probably obscene, but their point is lost; sailors cross-
ing the *line* or equator proverbially lost their hair from scurvy)   238 *by line
and level* according to rule (with pun on *line*); *an't like* if it please   242–43
pass of pate sally of wit

Speaks poetry
Nobel Character

TRINCULO Monster, come put some lime upon your 244
   fingers, and away with the rest.

CALIBAN
   I will have none on't. We shall lose our time
   And all be turned to barnacles, or to apes   247
   With foreheads villainous low.

STEPHANO Monster, lay-to your fingers: help to bear
   this away where my hogshead of wine is, or I'll turn
   you out of my kingdom. Go to, carry this.

TRINCULO And this.

STEPHANO Ay, and this.

    A noise of hunters heard. Enter divers Spirits in shape
    of dogs and hounds, hunting them about, Prospero and
    Ariel setting them on.

PROSPERO Hey, Mountain, hey!

ARIEL Silver! there it goes, Silver!

PROSPERO Fury, Fury! There, Tyrant, there! Hark,
   hark!

    [Caliban, Stephano, and Trinculo are driven out.]
   Go, charge my goblins that they grind their joints
   With dry convulsions, shorten up their sinews   258
   With agèd cramps, and more pinch-spotted make them   259
   Than pard or cat o' mountain.   260

ARIEL   Hark, they roar!

PROSPERO
   Let them be hunted soundly. At this hour
   Lie at my mercy all mine enemies.
   Shortly shall all my labors end, and thou
   Shalt have the air at freedom. For a little,
   Follow, and do me service.   *Exeunt.*

                       ❋

244 *lime* birdlime (sticky, hence appropriate for stealing)   247 *barnacles*
geese   258 *dry* (resulting from deficiency of 'humors' or bodily liquids)
259 *agèd* i.e. such as old people have   260 *pard or cat o' mountain* leopard
or catamount

V, i   *Enter Prospero in his magic robes, and Ariel.*

PROSPERO
Now does my project gather to a head.

2   My charms crack not, my spirits obey, and time
Goes upright with his carriage. How's the day?

ARIEL
On the sixth hour, at which time, my lord,
You said our work should cease.

PROSPERO   I did say so
When first I raised the tempest. Say, my spirit,
How fares the King and's followers?

ARIEL   Confined together
In the same fashion as you gave in charge,
Just as you left them – all prisoners, sir,

10   In the line grove which weather-fends your cell.

11   They cannot budge till your release. The King,
His brother, and yours abide all three distracted,
And the remainder mourning over them,
Brimful of sorrow and dismay; but chiefly
Him that you termed, sir, the good old Lord Gonzalo.
His tears run down his beard like winter's drops

17   From eaves of reeds. Your charm so strongly works 'em,
That if you now beheld them, your affections
Would become tender.

PROSPERO   Dost thou think so, spirit?

ARIEL
Mine would, sir, were I human.

PROSPERO   And mine shall.
Hast thou, which art but air, a touch, a feeling
Of their afflictions, and shall not myself,

23   One of their kind, that relish all as sharply
Passion as they, be kindlier moved than thou art?
Though with their high wrongs I am struck to th' quick,

V, i Before Prospero's cell   2–3 *time . . . carriage* time's burden is light   10
weather-fends protects from the weather   11 *till your release* until you
release them   17 *eaves of reeds* i.e. a thatched roof   23 *relish* feel; *all* quite

Yet with my nobler reason 'gainst my fury
Do I take part. The rarer action is
In virtue than in vengeance. They being penitent,
The sole drift of my purpose doth extend
Not a frown further. Go, release them, Ariel.
My charms I'll break, their senses I'll restore,
And they shall be themselves.

ARIEL   I'll fetch them, sir.   *Exit.*

PROSPERO
Ye elves of hills, brooks, standing lakes, and groves,
And ye that on the sands with printless foot
Do chase the ebbing Neptune, and do fly him
When he comes back; you demi-puppets that   36
By moonshine do the green sour ringlets make,
Whereof the ewe not bites; and you whose pastime
Is to make midnight mushrumps, that rejoice   39
To hear the solemn curfew; by whose aid
(Weak masters though ye be) I have bedimmed   41
The noontide sun, called forth the mutinous winds,
And 'twixt the green sea and the azured vault
Set roaring war; to the dread rattling thunder
Have I given fire and rifted Jove's stout oak   45
With his own bolt; the strong-based promontory
Have I made shake and by the spurs plucked up   47
The pine and cedar; graves at my command
Have waked their sleepers, oped, and let 'em forth
By my so potent art. But this rough magic
I here abjure; and when I have required   51
Some heavenly music (which even now I do)
To work mine end upon their senses that   53
This airy charm is for, I'll break my staff,
Bury it certain fathoms in the earth,
And deeper than did ever plummet sound
I'll drown my book.

36 *demi-puppets* i.e. fairies   39 *mushrumps* mushrooms   41 *masters* forces
45 *rifted* split   47 *spurs* roots   51 *required* asked for   53 *their senses that*
the senses of those whom

Solemn music.
Here enters Ariel before ; then Alonso, with a frantic
gesture, attended by Gonzalo ; Sebastian and
Antonio in like manner, attended by Adrian and
Francisco. They all enter the circle which Prospero
had made, and there stand charmed ; which Prospero
observing, speaks.

58   A solemn air, and the best comforter
     To an unsettled fancy, cure thy brains,
     Now useless, boiled within thy skull ! There stand,
     For you are spell-stopped.
     Holy Gonzalo, honorable man,
63   Mine eyes, ev'n sociable to the show of thine,
64   Fall fellowly drops. The charm dissolves apace ;
     And as the morning steals upon the night,
     Melting the darkness, so their rising senses
     Begin to chase the ignorant fumes that mantle
     Their clearer reason. O good Gonzalo,
     My true preserver, and a loyal sir
70   To him thou follow'st, I will pay thy graces
     Home both in word and deed. Most cruelly
     Didst thou, Alonso, use me and my daughter.
     Thy brother was a furtherer in the act.
     Thou art pinched for't now, Sebastian. Flesh and blood,
     You, brother mine, that entertained ambition,
76   Expelled remorse and nature ; who, with Sebastian
     (Whose inward pinches therefore are most strong),
     Would here have killed your king, I do forgive thee,
     Unnatural though thou art. Their understanding
     Begins to swell, and the approaching tide
     Will shortly fill the reasonable shore,
     That now lies foul and muddy. Not one of them
     That yet looks on me or would know me. Ariel,
     Fetch me the hat and rapier in my cell.

58 *and* i.e. which is 63 *sociable* sympathetic; *show* sight 64 *Fall* let fall
70 *graces* favors 76 *remorse* pity; *nature* natural feeling

I will discase me, and myself present   85
As I was sometime Milan. Quickly, spirit!   86
Thou shalt ere long be free.

> [*Exit Ariel and returns immediately.*]
>
> *Ariel sings and helps to attire him.*
>
> Where the bee sucks, there suck I;
> In a cowslip's bell I lie;
> There I couch when owls do cry.
> On the bat's back I do fly
> After summer merrily.
> Merrily, merrily shall I live now
> Under the blossom that hangs on the bough.

PROSPERO
Why, that's my dainty Ariel! I shall miss thee,
But yet thou shalt have freedom; so, so, so.
To the King's ship, invisible as thou art!
There shalt thou find the mariners asleep
Under the hatches. The master and the boatswain
Being awake, enforce them to this place,
And presently, I prithee.   101

ARIEL
I drink the air before me, and return   102
Or ere your pulse twice beat.   *Exit.*

GONZALO
All torment, trouble, wonder, and amazement
Inhabits here. Some heavenly power guide us
Out of this fearful country!
PROSPERO   Behold, sir King,
The wrongèd Duke of Milan, Prospero.
For more assurance that a living prince
Does now speak to thee, I embrace thy body,
And to thee and thy company I bid
A hearty welcome.
ALONSO   Whe'r thou be'st he or no,

85 *discase* undress   86 *sometime Milan* when I was Duke of Milan   101
presently right away   102 *drink the air* i.e. consume space

112   Or some enchanted trifle to abuse me,
       As late I have been, I not know. Thy pulse
       Beats, as of flesh and blood ; and, since I saw thee,
       Th' affliction of my mind amends, with which,
116   I fear, a madness held me. This must crave
117   (An if this be at all) a most strange story.
       Thy dukedom I resign and do entreat
       Thou pardon me my wrongs. But how should Prospero
       Be living and be here ?
PROSPERO   First, noble friend,
       Let me embrace thine age, whose honor cannot
       Be measured or confined.
GONZALO   Whether this be
       Or be not, I'll not swear.
PROSPERO   You do yet taste
124   Some subtleties o' th' isle, that will not let you
       Believe things certain. Welcome, my friends all.
            [Aside to Sebastian and Antonio]
       But you, my brace of lords, were I so minded,
127   I here could pluck his Highness' frown upon you,
128   And justify you traitors. At this time
       I will tell no tales.
SEBASTIAN [aside] The devil speaks in him.
PROSPERO   No.
       For you, most wicked sir, whom to call brother
       Would even infect my mouth, I do forgive
       Thy rankest fault – all of them ; and require
       My dukedom of thee, which perforce I know
       Thou must restore.
ALONSO   If thou beest Prospero,
       Give us particulars of thy preservation ;
       How thou hast met us here, who three hours since
       Were wracked upon this shore ; where I have lost

112 *trifle* trick; *abuse* deceive   116 *crave* require   117 *An if … all* if this is
really happening   124 *subtleties* (secondary meaning of) elaborate pastries
representing allegorical figures, used in banquets and pageants   127 *pluck*
pull down   128 *justify* prove

(How sharp the point of this remembrance is!)
My dear son Ferdinand.
PROSPERO   I am woe for't, sir.   139
ALONSO
Irreparable is the loss, and patience
Says it is past her cure.
PROSPERO   I rather think
You have not sought her help, of whose soft grace
For the like loss I have her sovereign aid
And rest myself content.
ALONSO   You the like loss?
PROSPERO
As great to me as late; and, supportable   145
To make the dear loss, have I means much weaker   146
Than you may call to comfort you; for I
Have lost my daughter.
ALONSO   A daughter?
O heavens, that they were living both in Naples,
The King and Queen there! That they were, I wish
Myself were mudded in that oozy bed
Where my son lies. When did you lose your daughter?
PROSPERO
In this last tempest. I perceive these lords
At this encounter do so much admire   154
That they devour their reason, and scarce think
Their eyes do offices of truth, their words   156
Are natural breath. But, howsoev'r you have
Been justled from your senses, know for certain
That I am Prospero, and that very duke
Which was thrust forth of Milan, who most strangely
Upon this shore, where you were wracked, was landed
To be the lord on't. No more yet of this;
For 'tis a chronicle of day by day,
Not a relation for a breakfast, nor

139 *woe* sorry   145 *late* recent   146 *dear* grievous   154 *admire* wonder
156 *do offices* perform services

Befitting this first meeting. Welcome, sir ;
This cell 's my court. Here have I few attendants,
And subjects none abroad. Pray you look in.
My dukedom since you have given me again,
I will requite you with as good a thing,
At least bring forth a wonder to content ye
171 As much as me my dukedom.
        *Here Prospero discovers Ferdinand and Miranda
        playing at chess.*

MIRANDA
Sweet lord, you play me false.

FERDINAND   No, my dearest love,
I would not for the world.

MIRANDA
174 Yes, for a score of kingdoms you should wrangle,
And I would call it fair play.

ALONSO   If this prove
A vision of the island, one dear son
Shall I twice lose.

SEBASTIAN   A most high miracle !

FERDINAND
Though the seas threaten, they are merciful.
I have cursed them without cause.
        [Kneels.]

ALONSO   Now all the blessings
Of a glad father compass thee about !
Arise, and say how thou cam'st here.

MIRANDA   O, wonder !
How many goodly creatures are there here !
How beauteous mankind is ! O brave new world
That has such people in't !

PROSPERO   'Tis new to thee.

ALONSO
What is this maid with whom thou wast at play ?

171 s.d. *discovers* discloses   174 *should wrangle* i.e. playing fair, as Ferdinand is doing, is not a test of Miranda's love for him

Your eld'st acquaintance cannot be three hours.   186
Is she the goddess that hath severed us
And brought us thus together ?
FERDINAND   Sir, she is mortal ;
But by immortal providence she's mine.
I chose her when I could not ask my father
For his advice, nor thought I had one. She
Is daughter to this famous Duke of Milan,
Of whom so often I have heard renown
But never saw before ; of whom I have
Received a second life ; and second father
This lady makes him to me.
ALONSO   I am hers.
But, O, how oddly will it sound that I
Must ask my child forgiveness !
PROSPERO   There, sir, stop.
Let us not burden our remembrance with
A heaviness that's gone.
GONZALO   I have inly wept,   200
Or should have spoke ere this. Look down, you gods,
And on this couple drop a blessèd crown !
For it is you that have chalked forth the way
Which brought us hither.
ALONSO   I say amen, Gonzalo.
GONZALO
Was Milan thrust from Milan that his issue
Should become kings of Naples ? O, rejoice
Beyond a common joy, and set it down
With gold on lasting pillars : in one voyage
Did Claribel her husband find at Tunis,
And Ferdinand her brother found a wife
Where he himself was lost ; Prospero his dukedom
In a poor isle ; and all of us ourselves
When no man was his own.

186 *eld'st* i.e. longest period of

ALONSO *[to Ferdinand and Miranda]*
                                        Give me your hands.
214   Let grief and sorrow still embrace his heart
       That doth not wish you joy.
GONZALO   Be it so! Amen!
       *Enter Ariel, with the Master and Boatswain
           amazedly following.*
       O, look, sir; look, sir! Here is more of us!
       I prophesied, if a gallows were on land,
       This fellow could not drown. Now, blasphemy,
       That swear'st grace o'erboard, not an oath on shore?
       Hast thou no mouth by land? What is the news?
BOATSWAIN
       The best news is that we have safely found
       Our king and company; the next, our ship,
       Which, but three glasses since, we gave out split,
224   Is tight and yare and bravely rigged as when
       We first put out to sea.
ARIEL *[aside to Prospero]* Sir, all this service
       Have I done since I went.
226 PROSPERO *[aside to Ariel]* My tricksy spirit!
ALONSO
       These are not natural events; they strengthen
       From strange to stranger. Say, how came you hither?
BOATSWAIN
       If I did think, sir, I were well awake,
       I'ld strive to tell you. We were dead of sleep
       And (how we know not) all clapped under hatches;
232   Where, but even now, with strange and several noises
       Of roaring, shrieking, howling, jingling chains,
234   And moe diversity of sounds, all horrible,
       We were awaked; straightway at liberty;
236   Where we, in all her trim, freshly beheld
       Our royal, good, and gallant ship, our master

214 *still* forever 224 *yare* shipshape 226 *tricksy* i.e. ingenious 232
several various 234 *moe* more 236 *trim* sail

Cap'ring to eye her. On a trice, so please you,   238
Even in a dream, were we divided from them
And were brought moping hither.   240

ARIEL *[aside to Prospero]*   Was't well done?

PROSPERO *[aside to Ariel]*

Bravely, my diligence. Thou shalt be free.

ALONSO

This is as strange a maze as e'er men trod,
And there is in this business more than nature
Was ever conduct of. Some oracle   244
Must rectify our knowledge.

PROSPERO   Sir, my liege,
Do not infest your mind with beating on   246
The strangeness of this business : at picked leisure,
Which shall be shortly, single I'll resolve you   248
(Which to you shall seem probable) of every   249
These happened accidents ; till when, be cheerful   250
And think of each thing well.
     [Aside to Ariel]   Come hither, spirit.
Set Caliban and his companions free.
Untie the spell.   *[Exit Ariel.]*
          How fares my gracious sir?
There are yet missing of your company
Some few odd lads that you remember not.
     Enter Ariel, driving in Caliban, Stephano, and
     Trinculo, in their stolen apparel.

STEPHANO Every man shift for all the rest, and let no
man take care for himself; for all is but fortune.
Coragio, bully-monster, coragio!

TRINCULO If these be true spies which I wear in my   259
head, here's a goodly sight.

CALIBAN

O Setebos, these be brave spirits indeed!

---

238 *Cap'ring* dancing for joy; *eye* see   240 *moping* in a daze   244 *conduct*
conductor   246 *infest* tease   248 *single* privately; *resolve* explain   249
every every one of   250 *accidents* incidents   259 *spies* eyes

How fine my master is ! I am afraid
He will chastise me.

SEBASTIAN   Ha, ha !
What things are these, my Lord Antonio ?
Will money buy 'em ?

ANTONIO   Very like. One of them
Is a plain fish and no doubt marketable.

PROSPERO
Mark but the badges of these men, my lords,
Then say if they be true. This misshapen knave,
His mother was a witch, and one so strong
That could control the moon, make flows and ebbs,
And deal in her command without her power.
These three have robbed me, and this demi-devil
(For he's a bastard one) had plotted with them
To take my life. Two of these fellows you
Must know and own ; this thing of darkness I
Acknowledge mine.

CALIBAN   I shall be pinched to death.

ALONSO
Is not this Stephano, my drunken butler ?

SEBASTIAN
He is drunk now : where had he wine ?

ALONSO
And Trinculo is reeling ripe : where should they
Find this grand liquor that hath gilded 'em ?
How cam'st thou in this pickle ?

TRINCULO I have been in such a pickle, since I saw you
last, that I fear me will never out of my bones. I shall not
fear fly-blowing.

SEBASTIAN Why, how now, Stephano ?

STEPHANO O, touch me not ! I am not Stephano, but a
cramp.

267 *badges of these men* signs of these servants   268 *true* honest   271 *her* i.e.
the moon's; *without* beyond   282 *pickle* (1) predicament, (2) preservative
(from the horse-pond; hence insects will let him alone)   286 *Stephano* (this
name is said to be a slang Neapolitan term for stomach)

PROSPERO You'ld be king o' the isle, sirrah?
STEPHANO I should have been a sore one then.   289
ALONSO
　This is a strange thing as e'er I looked on.
PROSPERO
　He is as disproportioned in his manners
　As in his shape. Go, sirrah, to my cell;
　Take with you your companions. As you look
　To have my pardon, trim it handsomely.

Gives Caliban more respect than the two drunks.

CALIBAN
　Ay, that I will; and I'll be wise hereafter,
　And seek for grace. What a thrice-double ass
　Was I to take this drunkard for a god
　And worship this dull fool!
PROSPERO   Go to! Away!
ALONSO
　Hence, and bestow your luggage where you found it.
SEBASTIAN Or stole it rather.
　　　　　　　　[Exeunt Caliban, Stephano, and Trinculo.]

PROSPERO
　Sir, I invite your Highness and your train
　To my poor cell, where you shall take your rest
　For this one night; which, part of it, I'll waste   302
　With such discourse as, I not doubt, shall make it
　Go quick away – the story of my life,
　And the particular accidents gone by
　Since I came to this isle; and in the morn
　I'll bring you to your ship, and so to Naples,
　Where I have hope to see the nuptial
　Of these our dear-beloved solemnizèd;
　And thence retire me to my Milan, where   309
　Every third thought shall be my grave.

Chooses time

Mortality

Land of living

ALONSO   I long
　To hear the story of your life, which must

289 *sore* (1) tyrannical, (2) aching   302 *waste* spend   309 *solemnizèd* (accent
second syllable)

313   Take the ear strangely.
        PROSPERO   I'll deliver all;
        And promise you calm seas, auspicious gales,
315   And sail so expeditious that shall catch
        Your royal fleet far off. – My Ariel, chick,
        That is thy charge. Then to the elements
        Be free, and fare thou well! – Please you draw near.

                                        Exeunt omnes.

Epi.   ✳ EPILOGUE ✳
                        spoken by Prospero.

                    Now my charms are all o'erthrown,
                    And what strength I have's mine own,
                    Which is most faint. Now 'tis true
                    I must be here confined by you,
                    Or sent to Naples. Let me not,
                    Since I have my dukedom got
                    And pardoned the deceiver, dwell
8   In this bare island by your spell;
9   But release me from my bands
10   With the help of your good hands.
                    Gentle breath of yours my sails
                    Must fill, or else my project fails,
13   Which was to please. Now I want
                    Spirits to enforce, art to enchant;
                    And my ending is despair
                    Unless I be relieved by prayer,
                    Which pierces so that it assaults
                    Mercy itself and frees all faults.
                    As you from crimes would pardoned be,
                    Let your indulgence set me free.   *Exit.*

313 *Take* captivate; *deliver* tell   315 *sail* sailing
Epi.   8 *spell* i.e. silence   9 *bands* bonds   10 *hands* i.e. applause to break
the spell   13 *want* lack

108

All Characters

freedom

Prospero speaks for all
       Freedom of
       ariel
       maranda
         ect.

Shakespeare

- It's his art
- Wants it to out live him

A Farwell
- applause

Coulesce

1st time he speaks as a man
              (human)
Celebration of
the man

FOR THE BEST IN PAPERBACKS, LOOK FOR THE

In every corner of the world, on every subject under the sun, Penguin represents quality and variety—the very best in publishing today.

For complete information about books available from Penguin—including Puffins, Penguin Classics, and Arkana—and how to order them, write to us at the appropriate address below. Please note that for copyright reasons the selection of books varies from country to country.

In the United Kingdom: Please write to *Dept. JC, Penguin Books Ltd, FREEPOST, West Drayton, Middlesex UB7 0BR.*

If you have any difficulty in obtaining a title, please send your order with the correct money, plus ten percent for postage and packaging, to *P.O. Box No. 11, West Drayton, Middlesex UB7 0BR*

In the United States: Please write to *Consumer Sales, Penguin USA, P.O. Box 999, Dept. 17109, Bergenfield, New Jersey 07621-0120.* VISA and MasterCard holders call 1-800-253-6476 to order all Penguin titles

In Canada: Please write to *Penguin Books Canada Ltd, 10 Alcorn Avenue, Suite 300, Toronto, Ontario M4V 3B2*

In Australia: Please write to *Penguin Books Australia Ltd, P.O. Box 257, Ringwood, Victoria 3134*

In New Zealand: Please write to *Penguin Books (NZ) Ltd, Private Bag 102902, North Shore Mail Centre, Auckland 10*

In India: Please write to *Penguin Books India Pvt Ltd, 706 Eros Apartments, 56 Nehru Place, New Delhi 110 019*

In the Netherlands: Please write to *Penguin Books Netherlands bv, Postbus 3507, NL-1001 AH Amsterdam*

In Germany: Please write to *Penguin Books Deutschland GmbH, Metzlerstrasse 26, 60594 Frankfurt am Main*

In Spain: Please write to *Penguin Books S. A., Bravo Murillo 19, 1° B, 28015 Madrid*

In Italy: Please write to *Penguin Italia s.r.l., Via Felice Casati 20, I-20124 Milano*

In France: Please write to *Penguin France S. A., 17 rue Lejeune, F–31000 Toulouse*

In Japan: Please write to *Penguin Books Japan, Ishikiribashi Building, 2–5–4, Suido, Bunkyo-ku, Tokyo 112*

In Greece: Please write to *Penguin Hellas Ltd, Dimocritou 3, GR–106 71 Athens*

In South Africa: Please write to *Longman Penguin Southern Africa (Pty) Ltd, Private Bag X08, Bertsham 2013*

The Pelican Shakespeare

_____	0-14-071430-8	**All's Well That Ends Well** Barish (ed.)
_____	0-14-071420-0	**Antony and Cleopatra** Mack (ed.)
_____	0-14-071417-0	**As You Like It** Sargent (ed.)
_____	0-14-071432-4	**The Comedy of Errors** Jorgensen (ed.)
_____	0-14-071402-2	**Coriolanus** Levin (ed.)
_____	0-14-071428-6	**Cymbeline** Heilman (ed.)
_____	0-14-071405-7	**Hamlet** Farnham (ed.)
_____	0-14-071407-3	**Henry IV, Part I** Shaaber (ed.)
_____	0-14-071408-1	**Henry IV, Part II** Chester (ed.)
_____	0-14-071409-X	**Henry V** Harbage (ed.)
_____	0-14-071434-0	**Henry VI (Revised Edition), Part I** Bevington (ed.)
_____	0-14-071435-9	**Henry VI (Revised Edition), Parts II and III** Bevington (ed.) Turner (ed.)
_____	0-14-071436-7	**Henry VIII** Hoeniger (ed.)
_____	0-14-071422-7	**Julius Caesar** Johnson (ed.)
_____	0-14-071426-X	**King John** Ribner (ed.)
_____	0-14-071414-6	**King Lear** Harbage (ed.)
_____	0-14-071427-8	**Love's Labor's Lost** Harbage (ed.)
_____	0-14-071401-4	**Macbeth** Harbage (ed.)
_____	0-14-071403-0	**Measure for Measure** Bald (ed.)
_____	0-14-071421-9	**The Merchant of Venice** Stirling (ed.)
_____	0-14-071424-3	**The Merry Wives of Windsor** Bowers (ed.)

_____ 0-14-071418-9 **A Midsummer Night's Dream** Doral (ed.)

_____ 0-14-071412-X **Much Ado About Nothing** Bennett (ed.)

_____ 0-14-071437-5 **The Narrative Poems** Shakespeare

_____ 0-14-071410-3 **Othello** Bentley (ed.)

_____ 0-14-071438-3 **Pericles** McManaway (ed.)

_____ 0-14-071406-5 **Richard II** Black (ed.)

_____ 0-14-071416-2 **Richard III** Evans (ed.)

_____ 0-14-071419-7 **Romeo and Juliet** Hankins (ed.)

_____ 0-14-071423-5 **Sonnets** Shakespeare

_____ 0-14-071425-1 **The Taming of the Shrew** Hosley (ed.)

_____ 0-14-071415-4 **The Tempest** Frye (ed.)

_____ 0-14-071429-4 **Timon of Athens** Hinman (ed.)

_____ 0-14-071433-2 **Titus Andronicus** Cross (ed.)

_____ 0-14-071413-8 **Troilus and Cressida** Whitaker (ed.)

_____ 0-14-071411-1 **Twelfth Night** Prouty (ed.)

_____ 0-14-071431-6 **The Two Gentlemen of Verona (Revised Edition)** Jackson (ed.)

_____ 0-14-071404-9 **The Winter's Tale** Maxwell (ed.)

The Penguin Shakespeare

_____ 0-14-070720-4 **All's Well That Ends Well** Everett (ed.)

_____ 0-14-070731-X **Antony and Cleopatra** Jones (ed.)

_____ 0-14-070714-X **As You Like It** Oliver (ed.)

_____ 0-14-070725-5 **The Comedy of Errors** Wells (ed.)

_____ 0-14-070703-4 **Coriolanus** Hibbard (ed.)

_____ 0-14-070734-4 **Hamlet** Spencer (ed.)

_____ 0-14-070718-2 **Henry IV, Part I** Davison (ed.)

_____ 0-14-070728-X **Henry IV, Part II** Davison (ed.)

_____ 0-14-070708-5 **Henry V** Humphreys (ed.)

_____ 0-14-070735-2 **Henry VI, Part I** Sanders (ed.)

_____ 0-14-070736-0 **Henry VI, Part II** Sanders (ed.)

_____ 0-14-070737-9 **Henry VI, Part III** Sanders (ed.)

_____ 0-14-070722-0 **Henry VIII** Humphreys (ed.)

_____ 0-14-C70704-2 **Julius Caesar** Sanders (ed.)

FOR THE BEST IN PAPERBACKS, LOOK FOR THE 🐧

FOR THE BEST DRAMA, LOOK FOR THE ⊕

☐ **THE CRUCIBLE**
Arthur Miller

Arthur Miller's classic dramatization of the Salem witch hunt, *The Crucible* is a chilling tale of mass hysteria, fear, and the power of suggestion.

152 pages   ISBN: 0-14-048138-9

☐ **PYGMALION**
Bernard Shaw

Shaw's portrayal of a Cockney flower girl's metamorphosis into a lady is not only a delightful fantasy but also an intriguing commentary on social class, money, spiritual freedom, and women's independence.

152 pages   ISBN: 0-14-045022-X

☐ **EQUUS**
Peter Shaffer

A deranged youth blinds six horses with a spike. A psychiatrist tries to help him. But what is help? *Equus* is a brilliant examination of the decay of modern man.

112 pages   ISBN: 0-14-048185-0

☐ **THE ACTOR'S BOOK OF CONTEMPORARY STAGE MONOLOGUES**
Edited by Nina Shengold

This unique anthology provides a wealth of materials for actors and acting students, and a wonderful overview of the best of recent plays for anyone interested in the theater.

356 pages   ISBN: 0-14-009649-3